The Wise Man In The Checkered Shirt

MICHAEL DRAKE

The Wise Man in the Checkered Shirt

Cover art by Rick Sutter.

Published by

SCRIBBLER
BOOKS
P.O. Box 511252
Salt Lake City, Utah 84151-1252

scribblerbooks@yahoo.com

ISBN 0-9713993-0-1 (First printed as ISBN 1-929281-07-2)

Printed in the United States of America
10 9 8 7 6 5 4 3 2

Prologue

Herod studied the face of his guest, this learned king from the East. He saw no fear. The fool hadn't even considered the loss of his own kingdom or power—not much of a wise man. It would be ill advised to take such a man into his confidence or disclose his own plan to destroy the infant infidel. He directed his chief priest to answer the man's question.

"The child should be born in Bethlehem, for thus it was written by the prophet: *Oh Bethlehem in the land of Judea, thou art not the least among princes, for out of thee shall come a governor to rule my people.*"

With a gnarled fist, the old king invited his guest to step forward. He clutched Melchior's wrist and pressed a gold coin into his palm.

"Go and search diligently for the child. When you have found him, bring me word, that I too may go and worship."

"Yes, good King, I will."

Melchior bowed a farewell. He left Herod at the garden fountain, and followed the guard back through the palace with its maze of chiseled halls. Outside the gate, he spoke to his waiting company.

"Gather and listen! The Child is at Bethlehem. Hurry, the day is nearly spent!"

The company traveled through Jerusalem then south toward Bethlehem until the sun touched the crest of the western hills. At sunset, they stopped to watch for the star that would soon illuminate the dimming sky. Once *it* appeared, Melchior left to climb a nearby bluff.

As the company prepared to resume the pilgrimage, Ben-Amalek paced at the foot of the bluff until he could no longer stand the wait. Finally, he bundled fruit and wine in a linen cloth and ascended the rocky slope.

"Lord, I bring your supper. May I provide assistance?"

Ben-Amalek spread the linen on the ground, but Melchior ignored him, engrossed in the image of Caesar on Herod's gold coin.

"No, my friend. I do not hunger."

"Master, all await your bidding. Shall we delay our journey to Bethlehem?"

"Is the Child at Bethlehem? We may have acted hastily. Herod knew nothing of the Child or the star until we inquired. We should follow the star, not Herod."

"Why then do we pause? Do you not see the star?"

"Yes, but I need to feel its light."

"I do not understand."

Melchior sat on the linen, then motioned for his servant to sit.

"When guided by the sun, do you follow its every movement? Walking east in the morning and west in the evening, you would end each day where you began. I do not seek for light that is seen. The blind man feels sunlight on his brow, and the star also imparts a light that may be felt. Now do you understand?"

Ben-Amalek hesitated. "I have felt sunlight, but I feel nothing from the star. *That* I do not understand."

Melchior gazed quietly at the star before answering.

"When the horizon first hides the setting sun, it no longer warms my face, yet I know its warmth within. That warmth remains even when all around me is dark. When again I see the color of dawn, the warmth within is renewed even before sunlight touches my face.

"Look again to the star, Ben-Amalek. It is too small to give warmth without, yet we may feel its whispered heat within. From *within* is how the light directs."

Ben-Amalek understood. He and his earthly master sat quietly on the bluff, seeking inner warmth and trusting the star would guide them to the Child of Promise.

Day One, Wednesday
Thanksgiving Eve

Jerome stood at the master-bathroom sink clad in crew socks, boxers and a red T-shirt, staring at himself in the mirror. The back of his T-shirt read *KISS ME BELOW THE MISTLE-TOE* with a cartoon mistletoe centered on his lower back.

After tracing his mouth with lipstick and dabbing inside the lines, Jerome pressed a folded tissue between his lips to remove globs. He puckered to make sure his lips were perfect and his teeth clean before swiping his forefinger across the lipstick and rubbing his cheeks a rosy red.

"If they could see me now," he said, thinking of his fellow elementary school teachers. He combed back his hair and sprayed it firmly in place before plastering blond eyebrows over his natural brows with heaps of styling gel. Rubber cement held better, but gel rinsed right off.

As he left the bathroom Jerome could smell the mothball and cedar scent of his red velvet suit on the bed. Black patent-leather boots and a curly blond wig rested on the cedar chest. Recalling *the incident*, Jerome marched to the dresser to rummage through the drawer for deodorant. He raised his arm and stretched his T-shirt to apply heavy touchup strokes.

He hated the spice scent. No respectable cologne had a spice aroma. When you smell spice, you smell deodorant.

Jerome returned to the cedar chest to finish dressing. Layer by layer he donned his gay apparel: figure-enhancing foam pads, red velveteen trousers and fur-trimmed coat, a wide shiny belt, the blond wig, a sassy red cap, and a beard.

Santa was ready to ho.

Jerome revered Santa as his Christmas profit. His and his wife's primary incomes didn't support his get-what-you-want-as-soon-as-you-want-it lifestyle, so he worked extra-curricular seasonal jobs. Mall Santas were paid on commission, earning 25% of photo sales during the shift. As the top photo-selling Santa, Jerome retained first dibs on the evening and weekend shifts that meshed perfectly with school and interfered conveniently with church.

Doing the Santa gig suited him fine—except for the children, particularly the spoiled kids he called "brats" and the soiled ones he called "rats."

Because photo sales mean everything in the Santa business, Jerome limited his interviews to three quick questions: *What's your name? Have you been good this year?* and *What do you want for Christmas?* A parental pitch always followed, something like: *Your child is so precious! How about a photo of this angel with Santa?*

Few parents could resist.

This year as always, the mall's North Pole opened on Thanksgiving Eve. Santa Claus made his grand entrance by jingling through the mall, waving and ho-hoing at disinterested shoppers. Mall security, like Santa's Secret Service, cleared Jerome's path by extending their arms to hold back the huddled masses yawning to writhe free.

Santa hoofed it to the escalator going down to center court where a flock of anxious children waited, tripping on the toothed-comb threshold of the escalator and chinking the jingle bells to a halt. Jerome teetered like a target-practice duck in a carnival midway booth, grasping at the handrail to regain his balance, then keeping a firm grip as he descended to center court.

The handrail moved slower than the escalator steps. Jerome pretended that his hand and his padded waist were in a horse race, neck and neck to the finish. The padding was about to overtake the hand for a photo finish when he noticed a young girl leaning over the round concrete fountain below. Her bare arm swished the water as she fished for coins.

"Get out of there!" Santa scolded as he rode the escalator past the fountain. The girl reeled in a fist of coins and twirled around. Water streamed off her bare arm, pooling on the floor around her dirty canvas shoes.

Using the traditional shame-on-you gesture, Jerome whittled his index finger in her direction. She stared back as she slipped her wet fist into a coat sleeve. When her fist wouldn't fit past the cuff, she dropped the coins into her other hand to finish shoving her arm into the coat. With one sleeve on, she burrowed the drenched fist of coins in her pocket, then stretched her free hand behind her back to nab the dangling sleeve like a puppy chasing its tail.

Jerome stepped off the escalator and strolled toward the girl, hoping for a reaction. She abandoned the dangling sleeve and scurried to a nearby bench where her toddler sister sat. The toddler pointed at Santa as her older sister dragged her away.

Chuckling under his beard, Santa turned to the North Pole to greet the throngs and take his throne.

"Ladies and gentlemen, children of all ages! Here comes Santa Claus!" bleated Moreen Goates into the microphone.

Moreen was the seasonal display coordinator, self-appointed as second-in-command to her brother and mall manager Werner Hilledge. She, too, received a cut of photo sales and was more than willing to work the children into a frenzy. She pressed her lips against the microphone to bray her rendition of *Here Comes Santa Claus.*

Jerome ho-hoed and waved his way to the front of the crowd, ending Moreen's performance by butting her away from the mike.

"Hello boys and girls!" he said.

"Hello," yelled the children in smeared unison.

Jerome put one hand on his hip, the other on his ear. "I can't hear you! Let's try again. HELLO BOYS AND GIRLS!"

"HELLO!" they screamed.

"Have you all been good this year?"

"YEAH!"

"Are you ready to visit Santa and tell him what you want?"

"YEAH!"

"Are you ready to get your picture taken with Santa?"

"YEEAH!"

"Then let's get to it!"

Making a Nixon-like wave to the crowd, Santa left the microphone to take his seat. His throne was nestled between two candy-striped poles on the porch of a fake-façade house with black-painted windows. Velvet ropes from here to Egypt channeled children to Santa's porch. The photo counter had been strategically placed near the velvet ropes so everyone in line had to watch giddy parents gawk at photos of their kids.

Child after child, sale after sale passed over Santa's knee. Between photos Jerome waved at the hordes of children to keep them entertained and in line. Parents appreciated the fast moving interviews. Santa appreciated the fast moving inventory. After about an hour, Jerome noticed the coin poacher and her toddler sister in line. The older girl now had both arms in her coat, her coin fist still buried in one pocket. Her free hand clutched the coat hood of the toddler who was dashing and dancing and prancing and vexing.

Both girls wore pants and coats they had outgrown. Their home-cut hair was uneven. They were maybe three and nine years old at most.

Jerome looked for their parents, but saw no one who fit the profile. The girls must have been dumped off.

Poster children for overpopulation, he thought. Malls and schools were not a place for unsupervised rats. He was neither a baby-sitter nor a probation officer.

As the girls advanced in line Jerome planned a reprimand for the young thief, reasoning that if her mom and dad weren't responsible enough, Santa had a duty to put her on the strait and narrow. The closer she got, the more he refined his reprimand and the less attention he gave to photo sales. By the time the last child in front of the sisters slid off Santa's lap, Jerome had the perfect reprimand in mind.

He opened his arms wide. The younger sister responded in kind, opening her arms and hopping up the porch step. She jumped into his lap, grabbing his coat fur to pull herself up.

The smell of upset tummy surged into Jerome's nostrils, making him turn aside to gasp for air as she squirmed for comfort. Caught off guard, he retreated from his planned attack.

"What's your name?" he wheezed.

"Man anus Boo."

"What?"

"She said her name is Boo," responded the older sister.

Jerome continued, breathing through his mouth. "Have you been a good girl?"

Boo nodded. "Uh-huh."

"What do you want for Christmas?"

"Iguana gad sum fin foe Hurries buff dye."

"All righty. Do you want a photo with Santa Claus?" he pitched, unable to resist.

"Uh-huh."

"Nuh-uh," corrected Boo's sister. "Not today."

Jerome scooted Boo from his knee, then reached for her sister. She stepped back.

"Aren't you going to enter Santa's confessional, young lady?"

"No."

"Where are your parents? You shouldn't be here by yourself."

"I'm not here by myself."

"Who's here with you?"

"Boo."

"Boo doesn't count. Where's your mother?"

"She's close by."

"You want to point her out? Is that her over there?" Jerome aimed a finger at Moreen to call the bluff. The girl shook her head.

"What's your name?" Jerome asked.

The young girl didn't answer.

"Don't you want to tell me all the naughty things you've done this year?"

"I don't talk to strangers."

"But I'm not a stranger, am I? I'm Santa Claus."

"Then how come you don't know my name?"

The astute observation stupefied Jerome. His brow furrowed as he looked down his nose at her.

"Touché. Would you like a photo with a stranger?"

"No."

Jerome grabbed four candy canes from the box by his chair as he glanced over to see Moreen watching him. She would not approve of him handing them out like candy, but he leaned forward to deliver them anyway, catching another unexpected whiff of Boo.

"Thank you," said the older sister.

"Fang ewe," said Boo.

The girls left the throne and stepped off the porch.

Santa sat back and rolled his eyes, lifting his mustache so the photography elf could read his lips. He wide-mouthed the word "rats." The elf smiled in reply, then darted behind the camera when Moreen approached.

"Easy on the candy canes, Tubby," she warned. "They don't grow on trees."

"Not south of Saskatoon," Jerome answered as another child climbed aboard his knee.

The sisters disappeared into a forest of shoppers, out of sight, out of mind.

Day Two, Thursday
Thanksgiving Day

Santa stood behind the classic Mustang convertible, leaning on the trunk and resting a boot on the tailpipe. He was careful not to let car exhaust creep up his pant leg, as he had no desire to die from carbon monoxide poisoning. The hot exhaust kept his foot toasty warm, a luxury he would not long enjoy.

Too cold for a parade, he thought as the marching band practiced to his side. A trumpeter blew a strand of insta-chilled moisture from his horn's spit valve as he stepped into formation.

"Atta boy," Jerome mumbled. He noticed his breath in the cold air and exhaled heavily with his jaw extended.

I should have brought a bubble pipe, he thought.

Mr. Hilledge sat in the driver's seat of the Mustang, crammed into his puffy goose-down parka and earmuffs. Moreen sat beside him dressed as Mrs. Claus, decked in red and wearing granny glasses. It didn't take many exterior alterations to make her look the part. Her body bulges were sufficiently large, and the costume-shop spray-on-rinse-out hair color simply restored the gray she already concealed with monthly dye jobs. She was the Mrs. Claus Jerome had always imagined, which was no compliment.

Werner pulled Navy sunglasses from his coat pocket and hooked them on his ears under the muffs. His berry-red nose made him look like W.C. Fields playing Admiral Byrd.

"Let's do it," he said.

"Ready, Nicholas dear?" crooned Moreen.

"Ready when you are, honey bunch. Tell you what, sugar plum. Why don't you hop in back with me?" said Jerome, hoping to use her as a wind screen.

"Oh, Jerome," she tittered. "I'm married."

Lucky you, thought Jerome.

"Lucky him," he said as he climbed over the side of the Mustang, slipping on a towel that Werner put on the naugahyde seat to prevent scuffs. He kicked the towel from under his feet and bellowed, "Okay Donner. Giddy-up."

Werner drove into formation behind the police motorcycle brigade and ahead of the high school band. When the police revved their engines, Werner revved his, squealing the fan belt.

The parade progressed in spurts, halting often for the entrants to perform. Every time Werner stopped for motorcycle figure-eights ahead Santa stood to shimmy and shake as the band played behind them. He did exaggerated adaptations of the hula, the twist and the monkey, anything to keep warm and annoy Werner.

Santa's dancing tested the limits of the Mustang's suspension. At each stop his behavior became more animated—never naughty, but hardly nice. Werner often turned to remind Jerome that the car was borrowed, but Santa's wild dancing resumed at every stop.

When the parade stopped in front of the mall, Jerome again stood to entertain. The marching band started to play *White Christmas*. The slow melodic tempo didn't accommodate Santa's dance style, so Jerome imagined an extra thump for every boom of the bass drum.

Santa oomphed his way through *may your days be merry and bright*, bobbing the convertible on its springs. The crowd jeered with whistles and catcalls. Werner complained more than ever before, demanding that Jerome immediately knock it off. The demands were ignored until Werner popped his foot off the brake. The car lunged forward, toppling Santa onto the trunk. The crowd laughed.

"Hey, Wiener! What did you do that for?" Jerome demanded.

The epithet had been heard. Werner's silence resounded above the brass instruments. He turned, lifting a muff from his ear.

"What did you call me!?"

Jerome swallowed the first excuse that crossed his tongue. It wasn't good enough. This would take some real dancing.

"Sorry, my face is nearly frozen." Jerome pressed his fingers through the mustache, and feigned phonetics as he rubbed his lips. "Waner, Whiner, Werner, Werner, Werner. There! Much better! Sorry if I got carried away. Just living the moment. This parade is the best part of my job. I look forward to it all year."

"I appreciate your enthusiasm, Jerome. But remember that we represent the mall, and we have to maintain at least a semblance of dignity."

"Yes, sir. I will."

"See that you do."

Werner turned back around and slowly drove forward as the motorcade finished its weaving routine. Moreen rolled her eyes at Jerome and gave a conciliatory wink. She was humored by the nickname Wiener, oblivious that Jerome had dubbed her Moron.

Pretty slick, pret-ty slick, Jerome mused to himself. He hummed the Oscar Mayer song as he waved to the crowd, until something caught his eye.

There they were, the two sisters, standing curbside.

Boo leaned forward and delivered two-handed clam waves to Santa, squeezing her palms open and shut as little girls do. Her face seemed to glow, perhaps because of Santa, perhaps because of the cold air on her cheeks.

Boo's sister ignored Santa, looking up and down the street. When the Mustang passed, the girls scampered behind it to cross the street in front of the marching band. Jerome rotated to watch them disappear into the crowd on the mall side of the street, again without their parents.

"That little weasel! She's going for more money!" he grumbled, almost leaping from the car to chase them even though the mall was closed.

For the rest of the parade, Santa danced no more than a light fandango. He couldn't get his mind off the impertinent scavenging girls. Even after the parade was over, he fumed in the back seat while Werner and Moreen chatted away.

"Thanks, Jerome," said Moreen when they arrived at the drop off.

"Thank you, Jerome," said Werner.

"Adieu," Jerome grunted as he jumped from their car into his.

He sped away, throwing gravel from his tires in a race to the mall, screeching to an angled stop at a red curb by the front entrance. He circled the empty mall on foot, checking custodial doors and delivery doors and every other door he came upon. They were all locked. He looked behind shrubs and checked ventilation grates but saw no sign of entry. Even so, Jerome suspected that somehow the girls had gotten inside and stolen coins from the fountain.

Jerome left the empty mall lot, turning left onto the parade-route street. Within two blocks he passed a chapel where people were building a full-sized wood-frame crèche on the front lawn. The air near the chapel was filled with the wonderful smell of roasted turkey, making him realize how hungry he was. He looked forward to gorging himself.

As he drove by the chapel, Jerome noticed its marquee near the sidewalk:

ONLY FOUR MORE SABBATH DAYS TIL CHRISTMAS

How lame. He honked his horn and waved, completely uninterested in whatever response he might get from the churchgoers. His eyes hugged the road, consumed with the thought of consuming mashed potatoes and cranberry sauce.

～⊙⊙～

Sitting on a front step of the chapel, Boo had seen Santa. She had waved back at him, but he appeared too busy to stop and say hello.

"Eye sore Samba Cloths," Boo told her sister when she came outside with a foil-wrapped plate of food.

"Yeah, right. Hold on to my coat and don't let go."

As instructed, Boo grabbed her sister's coat and held tight as they walked toward home with a cold turkey dinner for their dad.

Day Three, Friday

With the school day off, Jerome had no reason to get up early but he did anyway. He had slept like a baby— awake every few hours, bothered by the idea of the girls breaking into the mall. He showered and dressed, ate leftovers for breakfast, kissed his wife good-bye, packed his Santa suit in the trunk, and rushed off to work a good six hours before his North Pole shift was to begin.

In spite of his early morning start, Jerome arrived at the mall long after it had opened on the busiest shopping day of the year. He parked his car and hiked from the crowded lot directly to center court to inspect the fountain for evidence of coin disturbance.

He circled the fountain in a twitching frenzy. All the coins were gone, every last penny.

He rushed up the escalator to the janitor's closet. The door was locked. He knocked and listened, then knocked again. Above his panting he heard noises inside, but no one answered. He pounded on the door.

"Hold your horses!" said the janitor as the door swung open. "What's *your* problem?"

"The coins! In the fountain! The coins are all gone!"

The janitor blinked a few times, maintaining a bland expression on his face. "The coins are gone?"

"Yes. All of them. Stolen!"

"Stolen?"

"Yes."

"By who?"

"By *whom*. By a little girl and her sister."

The janitor blinked a few more times. He scratched the back of his thigh. "And *whom* are you?"

"I'm Jerome, the afternoon Santa."

At first the janitor showed no emotion, then visible fury rose from his stiff jaw to the top of his hairless head. His eyebrows angled downward, and his oversized, floor-mopping hands curled into tight fists.

"Did they take my brass spigots?"

"No. I don't think so."

"How about the water? Did they take my water?"

"No. It's still there. They just took the money."

"Those idiots in security! I knew this was going to happen! We've got to check this out, PDQ. Let's go! Show me where the fountain is!"

The janitor lurched from the doorway. Jerome darted ahead without noticing that the janitor pulled back to let him run wild and free. He was well down the corridor before he realized he was racing alone.

Laughter filled his ears. He skidded to a stop and turned to see the janitor bent over holding his sides.

When the janitor regained some control, he looked at Jerome and lost it again. Curious shoppers formed a large loop around them to stare. Jerome wished he were hidden inside the Santa suit. It took a while for the janitor to suppress his laughter.

"What a dork! I cleaned the fountain this morning!" He mimicked Jerome's frantic report, complete with gestures. "The coins! In the fountain! The coins are gone!" This made him laugh all the more.

Hot faced, Jerome ducked into the crowd. He hadn't felt this humiliated since the time the principal promised he would be the school's nominee for State Teacher of the Year, and at the PTA meeting he stood as the principal announced someone else. The principal didn't have the courtesy to tell Jerome in advance that, because *the incident* was under investigation, his nomination had been withdrawn. When the replacement nominee actually won the State award, it left a wound that still festered.

Jerome returned to the fountain and sat on its rim, seeking solace from the bubbling water. The pebbled surface impressed his underside so he tried his hands as cushions, making red pocks on his palms.

For the rest of the morning and into the afternoon he sat and sulked and watched people toss more coins into the water. Some closed their eyes when they wished, some mouthed words that Jerome could read. All of them flipped their coins into the air before their wishes plunked into the fountain.

Jerome was angry with the girls for his embarrassment even though he knew he had brought it upon himself. He stood and dug a penny from his pocket.

"I wish I were a fish," he said, flipping the penny high into the air. It came down, chinked off the fountain rim and rolled across the floor.

"Great," was all he could say.

He retrieved the Santa suit from his car and dressed in a stall of the lower-level rest room. Even with the beard covering his face, Jerome felt emotionally exposed, like an emperor in new clothes.

Day Four, Saturday

wo battered mattresses lay side by side on the linoleum floor of the one room, one bath apartment. The once glossy surface of the decades-old flooring was worn with brown trails. The sisters shared the better of the two mattresses that their father had salvaged, scrubbed and sanitized as best he could. The girls also had the luxury of a sheet and two blankets, either of which was better than the one on their father's bed.

The muffled alarm of the wind-up clock was barely audible through the folded towel draped over it. Bill quickly slapped the towel to shut off the alarm as he glanced over to see his oldest daughter press her eyelids closed, pretending to remain asleep. Boo didn't have to pretend. She cuddled Baby Bear in peaceful slumber.

Bill always slept in jeans to make his morning preparations easier. He pushed aside his blanket and wriggled to the mattress edge, anticipating pain with each movement. He rolled onto his left knee and dragged himself to the chair by the window, putting his forearms on the seat to heft himself up. He clenched his teeth as he scooted his weak right leg into position.

Steadying himself with the chair, Bill removed the leaning cardboard curtain from the second-story apartment's only window. The street lamp below the window cast the shadow of his head across the ceiling to the other side of the room. He ducked from the light to strap the canvas and fiberglass brace around his right leg, resting against the wall for balance and squinting in the dim light to see the loops and laces.

Boo snorted, startling her sister.

Bill glanced over, but he continued dressing without speaking. He pulled a sweatshirt over his head, then finger-combed his hair.

He took the aluminum crutches from the wall and slid his arms into the cold metal hoops, flexing and extending his forearms for a more comfortable fit before hobbling barefoot to the bathroom. Out of habit he reached for the light switch, but stopped when he remembered the power had been shut off. He left the door ajar to let streetlight enter the otherwise dark bathroom.

The young girl stared at the light streak on the ceiling. It ebbed and waned as car headlights passed the apartment building. Plaster cracks and crevices etched shadowy mountains and canyons. The bathroom faucet provided the placid sound of a gurgling stream, while the radiator crackled like a campfire.

She closed her eyes to see her mother making bologna sandwiches beside a picnic table covered with an old sheet. The breeze danced with her mother's hair. She could smell the potato chips and potato salad, and taste the mayonnaise and mustard on hoagie rolls.

Reflections of picnicking turned to remembrances of their comfortable house, again with thoughts of mother and food. Waffles, cakes, cookies, eggs, lasagna, spaghetti and hot dogs.

All served by mom.

All delicious and satisfying.

All swept away when her father cleared his throat, returning her thoughts to reality.

She blinked and slipped from bed, re-tucking the blankets around Boo's neck. The linoleum was cold on her bare feet as she scurried across the darkened room to the radiator. Although the apartment had been without electricity for weeks, radiant heat from the basement boiler was part of the prepaid weekly rent. Dark was better than cold. As she rotated the radiator handle, pipes creaked with the flow of hot water.

She didn't wait to warm herself but went to the corner and opened a large box on the floor, feeling inside for the last of the bread. She made two peanut-butter sans jelly sandwiches before emptying the bag of the last three slices of bread, one a heel. She set them on the table to wrap the two completed sandwiches in the bag.

The young girl squinted to look in the box again even though she knew there was nothing more to add to the meager lunch. She considered separating raisins from bran flakes, but there wasn't enough time. Instead, she opened the sack at the head of her mattress and got the stick-of-gum turkey she had made at school. She slid the foil-wrapped gum from the turkey, undid the bread bag and dropped it in, only to take it back out. She returned a half-stick to the bag as her father emerged from the bathroom.

"Good morning, honey," he whispered. "Sorry I woke you up."

"You didn't wake me up. The clock did," she whispered back. "Are you ready for your shoes?"

"Yes ma'am, I am." Bill huffed with the crutches to the chair, leaning to his left to take weight off his stiffened right ankle as he eased into the seat. She knelt beside and slipped a stocking over his toes, tugging it past the arch of his foot.

"How about doing *This Little Piggy?*" he joked.

She feigned a smile. "I washed your socks, but they're still wet."

"They're okay. They're not bad," he answered, tussling her hair. "I can't believe how grown up you are."

His daughter glanced up, then returned to the task at hand. She lifted his pant leg, exposing frowny surgical scars on each side of his ankle. She smoothed bunches of sock over his heel up to the leg brace, then doubled it down to the ankle before picking up his shoe. The leather at the big toe was shredded and the sole was worn smooth.

"You need new shoes, daddy."

"Too much ballet."

She feigned another smile. "The bottom is slick. You need new shoes."

"*You* need new shoes. We'll see if we can get you some for Christmas, okay?"

"I'm all right. Maybe for Marci."

"Okay. Maybe for Marci."

She tied the lace with a double knot, then moved to his other side to put on his left shoe.

"Want some breakfast?" she asked as she finished tying the laces. "There's some raisin bran."

"No. I'm okay."

"I can put some in a bag or something."

"No. I need to get going."

"Need help up?"

"No. Just a kiss. Here, give this one to Boo first."

Bill kissed her nose, then steered her toward sleeping Boo. She delivered the kiss, then returned for her own.

He took her hand. "Do you want a pig kiss?"

"No."

"A horse kiss?"

"No."

"A daddy kiss?"

"Yeah."

He obliged, holding her cheek in his hand.

"I should be home early, around three o'clock. Take care of Boo. And stay home. If you have any trouble, go see Mrs. Dixon." He raised himself onto the crutches, then made for the door. "You be good. I love you."

"I love you, too, daddy. I made you lunch," she said, holding out the bagged sandwiches.

Bill looked at the drying bread on the table and at the box in the corner.

"Is there enough left for you and Boo?"

"Yeah, there's enough."

"What's left?"

"Three breads, and peanut butter, and some raisin bran. And gum."

With her confirmation Bill accepted the bag, dangling it from the crutch handle. It swung back and forth as he hobbled through the door she pulled open. She waved through the gap and locked the door behind him.

He was gone again.

Boo was still asleep.

She was alone.

She listened to her father shuffle down the stairs, through the building entrance and into the early morning darkness. She stood on a chair at the window to see him, if she could, pressing her cheek against the cold pane. She stayed at the window long enough to watch the dark sky bleed to blue, then she got into her father's bed to resume her picnic at the ceiling mountains.

After the beds were made and Boo was bathed and dressed, the girls looked in the big box for breakfast. The unwrapped bread on the table was getting crusty.

"Boo, today we're going on a picnic. So, we're going to eat lunch for breakfast, and breakfast for lunch. I'll be the mom and you be the little girl. Okay?"

"Oat a."

The mom got the bread, peanut butter and a knife. She and her little girl sat on the mattress.

"Do you want a baloney sandwich?" asked the mom.

The little girl nodded *yes*.

The mom scooped a load of peanut butter and smeared it on a slice of bread. "Do you want mayonnaise on your baloney?"

The little girl nodded *yes*.

The mom smeared another load of peanut butter on the bread, then she wiped the knife on the lip of the jar. She folded the bread in half. "Here you go."

"Finks."

"You're welcome."

The mom handed the little girl the remaining half-stick of gum. "Here's a cookie for dessert. You want some punch?"

The little girl took a bite of the sandwich, nodded yes, and said a gooey "Uh-huh."

The mom filled cups of water at the bathroom sink. "Don't spill," she said as she gave a cup to Boo. She then made a sandwich for herself with the last of the bread.

A delivery truck in the street clattered by.

"Did you hear that?" the mom asked with googly eyes. "Did you hear the bear fall out of a tree?" She pointed to Baby Bear on the floor.

Boo got bug-eyed when she heard another thump.

"There. There it is again. Listen. Maybe it's an avalanche."

The radiator hissed.

"Do you hear the bird? Up there, in the tree."

The mother and daughter played in the forest for the rest of the morning, exploring it from corner to corner. They spelunked in a dark cave of porcelain pools and waterfalls. They navigated the river on a coil-spring raft. They climbed trees, spit from cliffs, ate bugs, chased moose, and roasted marshmallows.

By the time they returned to base camp the girls were famished and fatigued. They munched dry raisin bran for lunch before Boo fell asleep on top of the mattress. Her sister untucked the blankets from the foot of the mattress to snuggle them up around her. She then went to the window and leaned on the sill to watch the world outside.

Her breath fogged the cold pane. She drew a simple face on the foggy glass: two eyes, a nose, and a straight-line mouth. She touched her nose against the nose of the drawing. Her breath clouded the face into oblivion.

She was alone again.

⌘

Santa squirmed in his car seat, perturbed at catching every red light on his way to the mall.

"Come on, come on! Let's move it!" he shouted at each signal, inching his car forward in anticipation of the changing light and romping on the accelerator the instant it went green.

Santa was late.

Santa was cranky.

Santa neither waved nor honked back at fellow motorists, no matter how much they bounced about in their cars. But when a teenager offered a digital proctoscopy, Santa returned the gesture.

Jerome was now pinned behind a slow bus. Diesel exhaust infused the fresh-air vent, making him choke. Even though it had the green light, the bus suddenly stopped at the last intersection before the mall.

"Come on, you idiot! Green means go!"

Jerome honked the horn with his thumb. The bus didn't move. The light stayed green.

"Move!" He honked again before leaning into the passenger seat to look around the right side of the bus. He could tell the bus doors were open, but no one was getting out. There was no apparent reason for the delay.

Cars in the lane to his left zoomed by, keeping Jerome pinned behind the bus. He honked again and again before leaning into the passenger seat once more. He now saw a man with crutches and a leg brace descending the bus steps.

Jerome pressed his hand on the horn for one long blast. The bus pulled away, entering the intersection as the light turned yellow. Jerome accelerated forward, but the light turned red before he could run it. He screamed in anger, and pounded on the dash as he braked hard. The car rocked on the shocks as it stopped with the front bumper jutting into the crosswalk.

The man with crutches began to cross the street, side-stepping around the bumper. He just smiled at the inconvenience.

"Idiot!" Santa yelled inside his car. "You stink!"

He honked the horn with a quick slap to startle the man, faking a friendly wave as the man hobbled by.

The light changed with the man not yet across the street, but he was out of Jerome's way.

Santa accelerated off to the mall.

Day Five, Sunday

Unable to sleep, Bill lay on his back studying the plaster on the apartment ceiling. With very little imagination the textures mutated into various caricatures with extremities like his own: contorted and crooked, less than whole.

Streams of early morning light trickled around the cardboard curtain, smearing the caricatures into a mosaic of shadows. Bill squinted to rearrange the mosaic into a portrait of his wife, but he had to close his eyes to see her face. Before long he conceded that the day could not be delayed, and pulled the blanket off his body.

His daughters appeared to be asleep, but he knew that only Marci really was. He crawled to the chair, got to his feet and tipped the cardboard to peek through the window, verifying that his surprise had not frozen overnight.

"Okay, girls. Wakey up. We've got church today."

The chilled air near the window made Bill shiver. He stood there, momentarily unsure whether to first strap the brace to his leg or put on a shirt. He reached for the brace.

"Come on girls. Up and at 'em. I got a surprise for breakfast, in the fridge."

His oldest sat up and surveyed the room.

"We don't have a fridge," she said.

"Sure we do. It's Mother Nature's fridge. You'll see when you're ready for church. Wake Boo, and get in the tub."

With a few nudges and tugs, Boo was navigated to the bathroom. The hot water faucet squeaked to half-flow, then came the cold water. The girls plopped into the tub with the water still running.

"Not too full! Turn it off when it gets to Boo's belly button, okay?"

"Okay." The water was shut off, confirming Bill's suspicion that it was already there.

"Is it too full?" he asked.

"No," they replied in near unison.

Bill tightened the last strap of the brace, then put on his shirt. He crutched to the radiator, adjusted the heat, and returned to his mattress. He made the bed using the rubber tips of his crutches, tucking the edges with the toes of his left-foot.

The girls giggled and swished. Bill paid little attention until he heard bubble blowing.

"Hey! Get your face out of the water! That's not very smart."

"But I have to wash my hair."

"Well, don't dip your face! Use the cup."

"Can I lay on my back?"

"No. Then Boo would do it."

"She's already doing it."

"Sit up, Boo! Now."

There was a quick slosh followed by tub waves.

"Oat a, Tatty."

Bill hobbled from the mattress, set aside the cardboard curtain and opened the window. A half-gallon of milk rested on the slanted outer sill. He nabbed it and set it on the chair before closing the window. Ice crystals had formed in the milk, making it slushy.

Bill had gotten a few groceries with the tips he received Saturday afternoon. He usually bought inexpensive non-refrigerated food, so it had been some time since the girls had milk at home.

He studied the carton and the table a few paces away. Perhaps he could hook the carton with a finger as he maneuvered with crutches to the table, or maybe hold it under his chin. He stuffed the cold carton under his shirt and hurried to the table.

Bill set bowls and spoons, then got a saucepan and shuffled to the bathroom to get hot water.

"Excuse me, ladies," he apologized. "I'll just close my eyes." He closed one eye, rolling his open eyeball all around. Boo laughed, but her sister drew knees up to her chin, embarrassed by a man's presence.

"Sorry," he said. "I'll hurry."

Bill turned his back to the tub and filled the pan half full. He hobbled back to the table, gripping the pan and crutch handle together. The water sloshed but did not spill before he set the pan on the radiator to keep the water warm.

He added oatmeal.

He hated oatmeal.

He left it to soak and soften.

ͼ⊙ͽ

Everything the girls owned they kept in sacks personalized with crayon drawings placed at the head of their mattress. They found and put on their best dresses, wearing pants underneath to keep their legs warm. After putting shoes on all six feet, the older sister dragged the chair to the table for Boo. She poured icy milk into two glasses while her father spooned oatmeal into two bowls.

"There are some sugar packs in my pants from yesterday," Bill said, pointing to his jeans by the bathroom door.

Boo raced from the table, returning with a handful of packets. She tried to open one by herself—she was a big girl now—but her small fingers couldn't tear the paper. Bill assisted by opening the packet, but he let her dump the sugar by herself.

Bill leaned against the wall to eat his mush from the pan with no milk or sugar. Without a single complaint, the girls gnawed on each soggy-outside-dry-inside oatmeal lump like bubble gum without tutti-frutti flavor. They all finished their breakfast, knowing the meaning of waste not, want not.

"Brush your teeth and get your coats. It's time to go."

The girls complied while Bill put on a second shirt. Boo tucked Baby Bear into her coat before her sister zipped it up. Then the girls followed their father through the door to the hallway stairs.

Bill paused at the top step as if at the edge of a pool, then step by step he descended, crutches before feet. The girls no longer had to be told to stay behind him, just in case he fell.

The air outside was brisk and humid. Low clouds obscured the sun. The frozen park lawn looked more like clumps of white heather than grass, and the sidewalks were slick from frost flakes scattered by the wind. Bill stopped to tie the hoods of the girls' coats, instructing them to keep their ungloved hands in their pockets.

Even with the long walk, they arrived at the church an hour before Sunday School. The girls' noses and cheeks were berry red, as were Bill's face, ears and hands. The girls scurried to the wall as soon as they entered the foyer, hovering over the floor vent to direct warm air up their pants. They rotated over the vent like game hens skewed on vertical spits. Bill remained with them only long enough to rub away the itchy tingle in his hands, telling them to stay put while he attended to his usher duties. He tested the sound system, and checked between the benches for litter, swatting bits of garbage into the aisle with a crutch tip. He wheeled the hymnal cases to the doors on each side of the chapel.

With these tasks completed, Bill returned to the foyer. "Okay, girls. You pick up trash in the chapel while I change the sign. After you pick everything up, I want you right back here at the heater. Okay? And be reverent."

"Okay."

"Oat a," repeated Boo as she scampered into the chapel.

Bill stood at the front door, looking at the marquee by the street to determine which letters he would need. He fetched T H E E from the closet and got the sign key off the hook before gimping out the door into the cold.

His drag-feet gait cut a straight trail across the frost-laden grass, his crutches poking round indentations on both sides. The resulting pattern resembled stitch scars. Bill unlocked the marquee's aluminum-framed Plexiglas cover and swung it open. He removed F O U, repositioned the R, and squeezed T H E E around it.

The message now read:

ONLY THREE MORE SABBATH DAYS TIL CHRISTMAS

Bill closed and locked the marquee, then turned to go inside. He stopped to admire the full-size Nativity scene erected in the center of the lawn. Life-sized plywood animals, shepherds and Wise Men stood around a timber-framed crèche that housed a ceramic Holy Family.

Over the past few months Bill had repainted the ceramic figures with vibrant realistic colors, but no one except his daughters knew of his deed. He had come across the faded glazed figures in storage, and took it upon himself to repaint them.

Bill admired how Joseph looked after Mary and Jesus, appreciating firsthand the anguish Joseph must have felt in caring for the Child under such meager circumstances.

He returned to the church foyer to find his daughters waiting quietly over the heat vent. He put things away, and entered the chapel with his daughters to choose a bench end where he could extend his right leg into the aisle. There the family waited for services to begin.

Day Six, Monday

Jerome sat in the empty classroom with a gourmet TV dinner on his desk. He never ate lunch with his students. He refused to eat the bland kid chow prepared by amateur school cooks, opting instead to bring his own lunch which he kept in his own small refrigerator and heated in his own microwave oven.

Besides, it wasn't in his union contract to be a lunchroom or playground monitor. The last time he volunteered he got into more career-destroying trouble than he ever could have imagined, so he now spent the noon hour alone. He had no interest in fraternizing with the turncoat teachers who had fragged him years ago, after *the incident*.

Teaching was no longer what he once thought it was. Students were disrespectful, parents disinterested. He was no more than a glorified babysitter whose wages were subject to the political whims of legislators. He received no honor, respect or money. The cattle call of elementary education had stampeded his pioneer spirit long ago.

The final nail in his attitude coffin was hammered into place last year when his assistant principal application was used as a coffee coaster by the superintendent during the interview.

Jerome had always wanted the best for himself and his wife, but mostly for himself. They drove the best cars money could lease. Their home was in an up-scale neighborhood with accountants and attorneys, though they were only able to buy it after his wife's father died. She had inherited enough for a significant down payment, even without selling her parents' old house which they kept as a rental property. Still, it wasn't enough. Without hierarchical scholastic connections, Jerome had to seek out-of-student-body experiences to keep up with the Joneses, but he hated being a teacher, he hated being a summer handyman, and he hated being Santa Claus.

Jerome sniffed the ricotta noodle on his fork before dumping the gourmet meal into the trash. He opened the desk drawer to look for noontime entertainment, pushing aside his backup deodorant stick to find a miniature yo-yo in his cache of confiscated loot.

At the end of each school day, Jerome aligned his class in single file at the door to wait for the final bell, coats on and backpacks in place. The instant it rang, the children filed through the door quickly and quietly, the classroom clearing almost before the ringing quit.

Jerome was in his car and gone before most teachers said their last good-bye. It wasn't that Jerome was in a hurry to be somewhere. He was just in a hurry to be somewhere else.

As was her usual practice, Moreen parked in a handicap stall near the rear entrance of the mall. She reached across her son's lap to rummage through the glove box to get the blue parking placard.

Moreen had gotten the temporary mirror placard last year by haranguing a DMV clerk when Scotty broke his arm. After his hairline fracture healed, Moreen trimmed the expiration date from the bottom of the placard and kept it for her personal parking convenience.

Scotty started to open his door.

"Wait a minute," Moreen carped as she looked around. No one was in sight. "Okay. We can go."

Scotty stepped from the car and waited for his mother to walk around to his side. He followed her to the mall, just an umbilical-cord length behind.

In spite of his eleven years, Scotty Goates had no sense of responsibility or reality. A true believer, he visited Santa at least three times a week to refine his Christmas order.

As Scotty and Moreen approached the North Pole, Jerome stood, dipped his knees in a curtsey, and pompously proclaimed: "Hear ye, hear ye. His Royal Majesty Prince Snotty, Earl of Our Lady of Goatedumb," making sure the royal announcement was beyond earshot of Moreen.

Scotty butted in the front of the long line of children as Moreen flashed her mall ID in parents' faces. She winked at Jerome and left.

"How you doing, Prince?" Santa asked.

The photography elf snorted.

"All right, I guess," Scotty answered.

"Have you been a good boy these past twenty-four hours?"

"Yes."

"Groovy. So have you changed your mind about what you want? Or do we have additional items to discuss?"

"No. I just came to talk. Mommy says I have to ask you."

Jerome smiled. It was about time somebody schooled Scotty on Santa.

"Ask me what?"

"Well, there are these kids at school. And they lied to me. And I told them it was a lie, and they laughed and told me to ask my mom. But she says I have to ask *you*."

Jerome was in nog heaven. He could think of nothing more enjoyable than this. He wanted Scotty to admit that he believed in a superficial being. Then he would deliver the fantasy-can-be-reality speech that begins: *If you truly believe in Santa Claus . . .*

"Ask me what, Scotty?"

Scotty's lower lip began to quiver. He was ready to cry. "These kids," he whimpered. "These kids . . ."

"Et cetera, et cetera. Get to the point."

Scotty lost control of his facial fluids and buried his flowing face in Santa's beard. Cheek-deep in whiskers, Scotty blurted his unintelligible story.

Santa pushed Scotty back. Polyester hair strands clung to Scotty's face. Nasal syrup clumped Santa's beard.

"Okay. Let's get this straight. These kids at school told you some disturbing news. They said talk to mommy. Mommy said talk to Santa. Now Santa says talk. So talk."

Scotty sniffed, sighed and stared at Santa's forehead. "These kids at school say I'm adopted."

Jerome's eyes revealed his total surprise. He had a prepared lecture on the eternal nature of Santa, but not one on adoption. He glanced at Moreen standing by the photograph counter.

You mindless twit, he thought before turning again to Scotty.

"Look at your mother."

Scotty did.

"Your mom loves you more than anyone else in the whole world. And I know you love her, too. Don't ask me how. But let me tell you something I learned from an episode of Bonanza where Little Joe found out he was adopted. Little Joe was weeping like a baby, just like you, but Mr. Cartwright told him something that I'll never forget as long as I live. He said, 'Little Joe. Shut up or I'll give you a reason to cry.' Then he told Little Joe that when Hoss and that other guy were born, he didn't have any say about what he got. Looking at Hoss, I would have to agree. But Mr. Cartwright told Little Joe that he got to choose him. Do you understand what I'm saying?"

Scotty shook his head *no.*

"Okay. Let's try this. I'm going to tell you the truth about Santa Claus. If you truly believe in Santa, . . ." In a fleeting moment of charity,

Jerome hesitated. "If you truly believe in Santa, you'll run over and give your big mother a big hug. Then you'll tell her to get her big Hoss over here immediately. Capisce?"

Scotty nodded, then rushed to Moreen. He wrapped his arms around her, and buried his sobbing face into her blouse.

Santa held out the palm of his hand to halt the next kid in line. He got the attention of Moreen, and did index-finger curls for her to come over. She left Scotty at the counter.

"Well, I see he took the news hard, but it's good for him," she commented.

"I told him I was his father, and I wanted him to join the dark side." Moreen laughed.

Jerome continued. "Do you even have a clue what Scotty wanted?"

"Sure. That's why I sent him your way. Kids can be so cruel."

"Moreen, Little Joe heard he was adopted."

Moreen gasped as her knees buckled under the weight of a guilt rush. "Oh, my," was all she could say.

"It's your turn now," Jerome said. "I schooled him on the birds and the bees, and that man and woman thing. You go tell him about Santa."

Moreen's lips tightened. Jerome pushed her firmly to get her moving. Once again an inept parent had wanted him to do the dirty work, but not this time. He returned to his throne and invited the next boy forward. He cruised through him and other waiting children, focusing on photo sales while faking individual attention. Whenever he made a sale, he made sure to have the kids look directly into the camera so they would stagger flash-blinded to their parents.

"Next," Santa bellowed holding out his hand.

Boo and her sister stepped onto the porch. Jerome hadn't noticed them in line. The older girl's right fist was burrowed into a damp coat pocket. No parents were in sight.

"Hello, Princess. Been fishing again?"

She stopped far from Santa's knee. "Hurry, Boo. Go see him."

Boo climbed aboard Santa's lap. She smelled better.

"So. Your name is Boo."

She nodded.

"What kind of name is Boo? Is that short for Booger?" he asked.

"What kind of name is Santa?" her sister retorted. "Is that short for Satan?"

"Look, Robin Hood. I'm entitled to ask Maid Marian about her name. That's part of my job. No name clarification, no candy cane. Capisce?"

"Capisco," she replied.

Jerome grunted, partially annoyed by her adept response and partially by his not knowing whether she had correctly conjugated her answer. He continued his buttery-bitter interrogation.

"Let's see. Let me guess. Your full name is Boo Radley, and this here is your good friend Scout."

Boo smiled.

Her sister remained silent.

"No, that's not it. Hmmm. Try this. Your father is Casper the Friendly Ghost."

Boo smiled and shrugged her shoulders, but her sister had heard enough.

"She was born on Halloween, so we named her Boo. Now give her the candy."

"I'm not done yet, Princess. I have a few more questions. Where's your mom, Boo?"

"Sheep haven," she answered, pointing up.

"Then next time tell your mom to come downstairs with you. I want to give her a piece of my mind. So. What do you want for Christmas?" he asked, knowing full well the unlikelihood of her getting what she wanted.

Boo sat up and leaned forward. "Eye needle glad sum fling foe Hurry."

"No problem. It'll be there Christmas morning, wrapped in a pretty bow under the tree when you wake up."

Boo grinned, oblivious to Claus's contempt. He capped his interrogation by asking if she wanted a photo with Santa while he pushed her away. She nodded *yes* as she slid down his leg.

Jerome reached out his hand. "Your turn, Princess."

"Don't call me Princess."

"Sure thing, Princess. What's your name?"

"I'm not telling."

"Fine. Have it your way. No name, no candy cane."

"I don't want a candy cane. Just give Boo hers."

"Only if you show me what's in your pocket."

"No."

"Should I call the police?"

She stared into his eyes, and decided not to call his bluff. "Come on, Boo. We don't need his candy."

"You know, Princess, maybe I should call the police anyway. How about that?" The threat made the girls skedaddle off Santa's porch and down the corridor. "I know where you live!" Jerome yelled at their backs.

Boo's sister stopped and spun around. She stomped back to Santa, Boo in tow.

"You do *not* know where we live! You've *never* been there!"

"Maybe that's because Santa only visits good little girls."

Jerome watched his words impale the young girl. Her eyes glassed over. She blinked back tears. A single tear trickled down her cheek. She let go of Boo's hand and wiped it with her bare knuckle.

"Boo's been good," she said. "Boo's always good." Another tear rolled down her cheek, following the same track as the first.

Jerome noticed the silent crowd around the North Pole. All eyes were on him. The deafening sound of *Jolly Old St. Nicholas* on the PA system made his ears ring. He felt instant remorse, not for his berating behavior but for the inglorious limelight that rested on him, center stage.

"Don't cry. Not here," he whispered. "Here, have some candy."

He shoved a handful of candy canes under her chin, but she rejected them and walked away. Boo stepped forward and snatched the canes, stuffing them into her half-zipped coat with a teddy bear. She scurried away to catch her sister.

The next kid in line stepped forward. Santa held his palm out.

"I need a break," Jerome huffed as he stood to leave the throne.

"I'll break it for you," muttered the photographer elf.

Day Seven, Tuesday

The young girl grabbed the bar on the seat in front of her and stood to reach the cable strung above the bus windows, giving it two good tugs. An electronic chime sounded as the sign illuminated: STOP REQUESTED.

She sat again, zipped her coat and gathered her things, sliding her pencil into the gap behind the binding of her math book before closing it on her worksheets. The bus pulled over at the next stop, one block past the church and two blocks from the mall. She squeezed past the knees of the stout woman next to her and shuffled out the back exit, jumping over the curb onto the park strip. The pneumatic doors hissed closed, and the bus drove away.

The brisk air nipped at her cheeks and ears. She put the math book between her knees to pull the coat hood over her head. As soon as the laces were tied under her chin she nabbed the book and ran to the church, cutting across the lawn to the side door. The sign on the door read:

DAYCARE
Matthew 7:7

She went inside, shutting the door behind her to keep out the cold, quick-stepping on her toes to warm her feet.

"Hello," greeted the red-haired teacher.

"Is Marci ready?"

"She'll be ready in just a minute. Is your dad with you?"

The daycare teachers always asked the same question. They knew about her father's disabilities, so naturally they expected that she, not he, would come to get Marci. Nevertheless, they wanted assurance that her father was close by.

"He's waiting at the bus stop," she fibbed. "It sure is cold out there."

"I know. Old Man Winter is here."

"Old Man Winter is at the mall, too," she responded.

Marci entered the foyer from an adjacent classroom. "Hurry!" she cried.

"Get your coat. We need to go, okay?"

"Oat a."

The red-haired teacher yanked a thin pink coat off a wall hook and held it upside down. Marci pushed both arms through the dangling sleeves as the teacher tugged the tail of the coat up and over her face, then

down across her back. In that instant the coat was on and ready for the
teacher to zip.

"We'll see you tomorrow, Marci. Bye bye."

"Weighs Bevy Bayer?"

"Oh, that's right! She's here in your cubbyhole." The teacher tucked
Baby Bear in Boo's coat and zipped, patting the lump. "There you go."

Content, Boo smiled and took her sister's hand as they stepped out
the door. They stopped at the sidewalk to look at the Nativity.

"Okay, let's go. We'll see Baby Jesus again tomorrow."

"Wee grocery Sand Claws?"

"No, not today. We'll go get Christmas money, but we're not going
to Santa. You'll just have to wave."

∽✺∾

Boo sat on the mall bench with the math book under her bottom.
Her sister sat on the edge of the fountain, trying to appear invisible,
waiting for an opportune moment to turn and plunge her arm into the
water. When she thought no one was watching, she rolled onto her
tummy to snatch a few coins, stretching her legs for balance. She then
flipped around a few cents richer, letting her coin fist drain behind her
back before dumping moist money into her coat and scooting to another
spot.

Boo watched the big man in white carrying a long stick. He had a
shiny head and looked like a friendly snow man. The long stick had a
funny little T on the end. His eyes met Boo's. The funny man winked at
her, then he looked at her sister bobbing for money. Quietly, he walked
to the fountain and stood next to the toe-down feet.

"Ahem."

Boo's sister spun around and jumped up. Water poured off her arm
onto the janitor's white shoes. She stood nose to navel with him, her eyes
drawn to the fabric divot over his belly button. She looked up into his
hairy nostrils.

The janitor cocked his chin down to look her in the eye. Without
blinking, he inspected her well-worn attire. "Is that your sister?" he
asked, tilting his head toward Boo.

"Yes."

"Is your mommy or daddy here?"

"My daddy's at work."

"How about your mom?"

She didn't answer.

The janitor glanced at the North Pole display. "Are you the girl who's been taking money from the fountain?"

She wanted to say *no*, but she knew the difference between little lies and big lies. She told little lies to get her sister from daycare only because her father never got home until after it closed. In her present predicament, anything but the truth would be a big lie.

She hung her head and answered. "Yes."

"Good. I've been waiting for you." The janitor took a quarter from his pocket and flipped it high into the air. "I wish you'd get this money out of my fountain," he said as it plunked into the water. He then held out the long-handled squeegee. "Here. Try this. You can sweep money to the edge. But leave the pennies. Those people need their wishes more than the others."

She didn't know what to say.

"Go on, take it," he coaxed. "Get those coins out of there."

Not needing a second invitation, she took the squeegee and within minutes had mastered the art of coin sweeping. She pulled money to the edge where it was easy to reach, particularly with the janitor standing guard.

"I'll leave the nickels, too," she decided aloud. "Those guys need their wishes, too." Soon both her coat pockets were packed with dripping quarters and dimes.

"All right, that's enough for today," said the janitor. "Save some for tomorrow." He took the squeegee and shook off the water while she put on her coat. She had to press her hands against the brimming pockets to hold the coins inside.

"Come on, Boo. Time to go."

Boo slid off the bench, exposing the forgotten math book. Her sister pushed coins deeper into her pockets to free a hand, then turned to say good-bye. The janitor was already far down the corridor.

"Thanks!" she yelled.

"You're welcome!" he hollered without turning or slowing. "See you tomorrow."

"Sea ewe tom arrow," yelled Boo.

ith the janitor by her side, the young girl stood boldly on the rim of the fountain sweeping coins with the squeegee blade. Boo stood at his other side, resting her elbows on the rim.

"Tan eye hip?" she asked.

"No," her sister answered. "You're too little."

The janitor interceded. "Tell you what, sweetie. When she gets the money out, you put it in the pockets. That way you won't fall in the water."

Boo stuck out her tongue at her sister.

"*My* pockets, Boo. Not yours."

The janitor suddenly grabbed the squeegee. "Here, my turn for a minute. Hop down."

He lifted her off the rim, then held the squeegee over the water. He immersed the blade and stroked it against the glass surface of an underwater lamp as Moreen and Werner walked by.

"Afternoon, Mrs. Goates. Mr. Hilledge," the janitor acknowledged with a genteel nod.

Moreen and Werner stopped to watch him scrape the lamp cover with the tip of the rubber blade.

"What on earth are you doing, Mr. Ludwig?" Werner asked.

"Well, sir, there have been complaints about mosquitoes," he promptly replied. "I'm wiping the larvae off the lights where they gestate."

"Mosquitoes? *I* haven't seen any mosquitoes."

"Thank you, sir. Kind of you to notice."

Moreen chimed in. "I noticed a few last week around the poinsettias, but I haven't seen any this week. Job well done, Mr. Ludwig."

"Wouldn't it be smarter to mix pesticide in the water?" Werner asked. "Why should we expend labor costs doing this?"

"Well, I wanted to go the pesticide route, but someone from management—was that you, Mrs. Goates?—told me not to, so we wouldn't kill any kids who put their hands in the water."

Moreen nodded, taking full credit for the non-existent directive.

Werner stood silent for a moment, mouth breathing. He abruptly turned to leave. Moreen followed.

"There used to be a time when the guy in charge was the guy in charge," Werner complained. "Nobody tells me anything anymore."

"I told you. You just didn't listen," Moreen countered, renewing their sibling rivalry. "You never listen."

"You never shut up," he retorted, flapping his arms as they argued down the hall.

The janitor sat on the fountain rim. "Don't try to get any coins unless I'm around. I don't want you to get in trouble. Got it?"

"Got it."

"Crawdad," Boo mimicked.

"Let's gather up what we've got and get out of here, then you can go see Santa. The line's not very long."

"No, thank you. We don't like him. He's not very nice."

"Well, you tell him that if he's not nice, the janitor will thump him upside the head, okay?"

"Oat a. Thumb hem up seed theater," Boo giggled.

"Right. Upside the head," he said with a grin.

Boo delivered the message to Santa. "Shoe snot knives, hem thumb ewe up seed theater."

"Huh?" asked Jerome.

"Thumb ewe up seed theater."

Santa looked to her sister for an interpretation.

"She said if you're not nice, the janitor will thump you upside the head."

Jerome bellowed a laugh, but quickly suppressed follow-up laughter as the threat registered. The message was sincere *and* serious. He searched the crowd until he saw Mr. Ludwig watching from the fountain. The janitor raised his large hand, and curled his fingers into an empty chokehold the size of Santa's neck.

Jerome waved back, message received. He lifted Boo onto his knee.

"Hello, Boo. Have you been good?"

She nodded.

"What do you want for Christmas?"

"Iguana tofu Hurries buff dye."

The request sounded familiar but was still unintelligible to him.

"Okay. I'll see what I can do. Would you like—" He stopped the sales pitch mid-sentence. "Would you like a candy cane?"

"Uh-huh."

He gave her a cane but kept her on his lap while he reached out to

Boo's sister. He noticed but ignored her bulging pockets, knowing that the janitor was still watching from the fountain.

"Did you want to see Santa?"

"No."

"You sure?"

"Yes."

He offered her a candy cane.

"I don't want it," she said. "I don't want anything from you."

Jerome retracted the cane while he helped Boo off his knee, then he held it out again, mustering a meager apology.

"Please. Take it. I want you to have it."

"No."

"Then I'll save it for you," he answered, hooking the crook on the furry trim of his pocket. "Whenever you want it, it's right here." He patted the cane and winked, glancing over to the fountain. The janitor saluted, but did not turn away until the girls left Santa's porch.

Jerome watched them wade deep into a wave of shoppers, without parents, without guidance. He couldn't comprehend why anyone would bring children into the world without accepting the corresponding responsibility.

That's why I don't have kids, he thought as he ho-hoed and waved to the children in line.

Day Nine, Thursday

All dressed up and no place to go, Santa waited in the rest room stall, using the toilet as a chair. The cheap plastic hinges on the horseshoe seat twisted as he shifted for comfort. Toilets don't make the best ottomans, but there were no other seating accommodations in the rest room/dressing area.

Jerome looked at his watch. Still ten minutes to his shift. He scooted forward a little, then leaned back against the tank. He stretched his legs and rested his feet against the closed stall door, tugging at his trousers to pull the fabric taut so it wouldn't dip into the water. Pillowing his head against the seat-cover dispenser, Jerome closed his eyes to nap.

The flush handle dug into his ribs. He arched a little and moved to the left. The plastic hinges creaked and suddenly cracked under the stress, throwing the seat sideways. His boots slipped off the door. Jerome grabbed for the roll holder, his shoulder blade hitting the flush handle just as his thigh plunged into the bowl. Water shot over his pants as he jockeyed on the horseshoe seat, desperately struggling to dismount.

By the end of the porcelain pony ride, Santa's back leg was soaked. He left the puddled stall to fetch paper towels and dry himself. He was at the trash bin dabbing his wet trousers when the ending-shift Santa came in.

"How you doing, Nick."

"Long time no see, Nick."

"A little trouble with your plumbing, Nick?"

"I slipped on a puddle left by the janitor."

The other Santa looked into the open stall. The broken seat and floor were splattered with water. A wet trail led to Jerome.

"I'll tell the janitor to wipe your puddles as you make them," Santa snickered.

"Hardee-ho-ho," Jerome countered as he brushed by him to leave the rest room. The wet spot on Santa's pants was now enhanced by specks of paper.

Toilet water still dripped down Jerome's leg as he walked crabways to hide the splash mark. He sat sidesaddle in the throne before calling to the first child in line, noticing that the two girls were only a few children back. He winked at them, aware that Mr. Ludwig was probably watching.

Boo returned two-eyed winks, but her sister pretended to study loose worksheets in her math book. She closed the book when they stepped onto Santa's porch.

"Hello, girls."

"Harrow, Sandy Clots."

"Hi."

Jerome spoke first to the older sister.

"I still have your candy cane." He pulled a moist broken cane from his pocket. It had not fared well during the plunge. Red and white crumbs rested at the bottom of the wrapper. "Whoops. I'll get you another."

"That's okay. Don't worry about it." She noticed Santa's wet spot. "Been fishing again?"

"Hardee-ho-ho. Are you going to tell me your name today? I promise I won't call the police."

"Are you going to tell me yours?"

"I'm Santa Claus. Right, Boo?"

Boo shook her head *yes*, but her sister shook hers *no*. "Yeah, right. That's why you have a fake beard, because you're Santa Claus."

"Well, maybe I'm Santa's helper."

Boo nodded again.

"Nope. Not true."

"Tell you what," Jerome offered. "I'll tell you my name if you tell me yours. Deal?"

She thought before responding. "Deal," she agreed.

"You first," said Santa.

"Nuh-uh. No way. You first."

"Fine. My name is Nicholas. My friends call me Nick."

She stared at him. His left eye twitched. She inhaled slowly before answering. "My name is Rumpelstiltskin. My friends call me Rump."

"That's a lie," Jerome complained. "You promised."

"You lied first. Lies don't count."

Jerome almost admired her wisdom. She reminded him of someone, but he couldn't place his finger on it.

"You're right," he acknowledged. "Lies don't count." He glanced at the math book in her hand. The top of the worksheet sticking out of the book revealed: *Name: H*—something. The rest of her name was covered.

He smiled under the beard. "Can I take a peek at your book? I haven't seen one like that for years."

He reached. She watched his hand take a hold of the book, then she, too, noticed the partially exposed name on her homework.

"No," she said, pulling back. "Let go."

Santa scooted forward to get a firmer grip. "Come on, let me see the book."

"No! Let go!"

He pulled the book toward him, dragging her along.

She screamed, loud and long.

Instantaneous crowd silence followed. *The Little Drummer Boy* from the sound system pounded on his eardrums. All eyes were again on him, frozen in time with his grubby mitt on the book.

He let go, rested his elbows on his knees, and cupped his hands against his temples. The tunnel vision left only her in his view.

"*Please,* don't scream. I don't need this." Jerome rubbed his wig for an extended moment. She broke the silence.

"Ask Boo what she wants so we can go."

"I already know what Boo wants," he answered. "She wants some mumbo jumbo dumbo bumbo."

"No, she doesn't. You don't really listen, do you?"

He took a quick breath to curtly reply that Boo didn't really talk, but instead held his tongue. "You're right. I should listen better. I'm sorry." Jerome couldn't believe he had just apologized.

"I'm sorry I screamed."

"I'm sorry I made you scream." Jerome couldn't believe he had apologized again. "Are you ready for a candy cane?"

"No. Just give Boo hers."

Santa gave Boo a cane, then placed two others in his pocket.

"These will be here for you when you want them. Deal?"

"Maybe. If you're good," she said.

"Hardee-ho-ho," he muttered as Boo waved good-bye.

With a quick nod, the elf directed Jerome's attention to the photo counter. Moreen stood there with her arms folded. She raised a hand and gestured for him to come. Santa held out his palm to stop the next child, then crossed the porch to her.

"Hello, Moreen. What's up?"

"I've been engaged in extensive discussions with the custodian. I want some answers."

"Answers about what?"

"About the little fountain problem we have."

Jerome glanced around for the girls but they were gone. "Look, no matter what they said, it's really easy to explain."

"So, it was you. I've half a mind to make you pay."

You're exaggerating, thought Jerome. *You don't have anywhere near half a mind.* He asked, "Make me pay?"

"Yes. I should make you pay, but the fact that you've admitted responsibility is admirable. Next year, use moth balls."

"Huh?"

"You heard me. Use moth balls. Mr. Ludwig says if you had used moth balls last year, we wouldn't have this mosquito infestation. There's no excuse for this, Jerome. No excuse at all."

"Mosquito infestation? I didn't infest this place with mosquitoes."

"Did you use moth balls?"

"Yes. Smell." He held out his sleeve for her to sniff, but she declined.

"Then buy a better brand. Now get back to work. The kids are waiting."

"Wait. Hold still," he said, staring at her shoulder before slapping her. "Got him!" He quickly brushed her shoulder.

"One more thing, Jerome. Control the children better, please. We don't want people to think you're torturing them."

"No, we don't want that," he said, adding "Moron" under his breath as he walked away.

Day Ten, Friday

anta reached into his pocket to retrieve the two candy canes. Both were still in excellent condition. He held them out as the girls stepped onto the porch. Boo's sister accepted them without a word. His wrinkled forehead revealed a smile under his beard.

"Hello, girls. How are you today?"

"Fine, thank you."

"Fun, fink ewe."

Boo climbed on Santa's lap.

"Hello, Boo. Were you good today?"

"Uh-huh."

"Read any good books?"

"Uh-huh. Bee Baa Woof ant Free Picks!"

Jerome grinned. He needed no interpretation.

"Who's afraid of the big bad wolf?"

Boo poked her pointy finger into Santa's padded chest.

"Okay, okay. Tell me what you want for Christmas."

"Eye waddle pleasant foe Hurries buffed egg."

Jerome's gift of tongues came to a sudden end. "Okay. Eye waddle, gada da vida, Ferrari puffed egg?" he mimicked.

Boo shook her head *no*. "Eye needle tofu Hurry."

"Eye needle tofu hurry?" Jerome repeated. "What's the hurry?"

"Don't tell him, Boo," her sister interjected.

Jerome was on to something. "Come on, Boo. What's the hurry?"

"No," Boo corrected. "Har-wee."

"Harwee?" he asked.

"I mean it, Boo," her sister threatened.

Boo giggled. "Nuh-uh. Har-*ley*!"

"Harley? Is that it?"

Boo nodded.

"You want a Harley?"

Boo shook her head and pointed at her sister.

"Your sister wants a Harley?"

Boo shook her head again, and pointed to herself. "Boo," she instructed. She then pointed away. "Hurry."

A low-watt bulb in Jerome's head lit up, refracting twinkles to his eyes. He gleefully joined in the pointing. "Your name is Harley!"

"It is not!"

"Yes it is. Boo says so."

Harley raised her fist at him. "No it isn't!" She then shook her fist at Marci. "You're going to get it, Boo."

"Now don't get all huffy just because Santa learned your name. Harley is an interesting name. It's a good name, better than Rump. I like it."

"It is not a good name. Don't you call me Harley!"

"Whatever you say, Rump. Would you like another candy cane?"

"No!"

"Would you like a photo with Santa Claus?" he teased.

"Heck no!"

"Then I'll see you tomorrow."

"No you won't!" she answered, her eyes teeming with anger. She turned her back.

Boo slipped off Santa's lap and waited with an open hand until she got her candy.

"You need to learn how to shut up," Harley scolded, squeezing Boo's hand as they walked away. Boo turned to Santa and delivered a parting two-eyed wink.

Jerome returned a two-eyed wink of his own.

Day Eleven, Saturday

Six days a week Bill woke before dawn to catch the uptown bus to a physical therapy clinic. The therapist allowed Bill free use of the clinic's exercise equipment, so long as he yielded to insured patients.

Bill recognized and appreciated the generosity, so he went out of his way to stay out of the way. He always arrived before the clinic officially opened, entering through an employee door using a key entrusted to him. Early in the morning he was able to use the high-demand equipment when there was no demand at all. As soon as paying patients began to arrive, Bill moved to the lesser-used equipment, eventually ending his morning workout in the pool.

The staff voluntarily assisted Bill with needed manipulation to increase his strength and range of motion. He thanked them regularly but not incessantly, knowing that true appreciation is expressed through action. He returned service for service. For each workout hour, Bill reciprocated with an hour of grunt work, cleaning handrails, scrubbing trash cans, dusting shelves, polishing knobs, and wiping light switches—things usually overlooked by night custodians.

Bill tried to leave by noon to earn whatever living he could. Public assistance provided bus passes and a meager monthly stipend, but it was hardly enough to make ends meet. In the past he went from business to business seeking odd jobs for a fair wage. Often business owners had offered small change without requiring work, but Bill refused pity cash.

The week before Thanksgiving he found steady employment sacking groceries at a supermarket, earning an hourly wage off the books plus tips—although most customers ignored his I WORK FOR TIPS badge. The work was strenuous for him, but it steadily improved his balance and coordination.

He stashed his crutches in the stockroom and scooted on a shopping cart to the front checkout stands, gymnastically using the cart handle and counter as pommel bars. Through each afternoon Bill conversed with customers to improve his chances for tips, but talk is cheap when the dialogue begins with "paper or plastic?"

Late in the afternoon Bill noticed a beautiful woman enter the supermarket. The sight of her made his pulse quicken. He studied her face as she pulled a cart from the line, then watched for her each time she rounded an aisle. He didn't gawk, but he was intrigued. She carried herself with grace and dignity, even in a supermarket setting.

From his wallet Bill pulled a photo of his wife and compared it with the woman. In most respects the woman was different, but something about the way she held her shoulders and the shape of her eyes brought back haunting memories. He put the photo in his shirt pocket and tried to think of something, anything, else.

The woman got in a checkout line two stands away. It would be patently forward of him to move from his present assignment to that stand.

A sudden crash startled him. He looked to the entry of his checkstand to see a boy, eyes bugging and ready to cry, with green juice, shards of glass and gherkins puddled at his feet. The checker made an intercom call for cleanup, then put a CLOSED sign on the cash register. She had the boy hook a chain from the tabloids to the gum as she redirected people to other checkers.

Bill hobbled over to bag groceries for the woman. She was even more beautiful at arm's length. Her face was flawless. Her simple but stylish clothes made him uncomfortably aware of his shabby attire. Everything about her was perfect, except for a finger on her left hand. It bore a wedding band.

"Paper or plastic, ma'am?" he asked looking away.

"Paper, please."

Bill noticed the woman's eyes on him as he sacked her groceries in doubled bags. He returned a polite glance and felt his face flush. He forced his chin down. He would look at her no more. His heart pounded arrhythmically, ready to burst. As he inhaled to relieve the pain, his breath rattled. Frantic now, he hurried to finish bagging her groceries before he imploded.

The woman paid the cashier and walked to the loaded cart.

"Thank you, ma'am," Bill said softly without looking up. "Come again."

"Thank you," she answered. "I will."

He felt the unexpected touch of her warm smooth fingers on his wrist.

"Whatever it is," she comforted, "I hope it turns out all right." She slipped a folded bill into his hand.

"Thank you," he whispered with effort. "Merry Christmas."

"And to you."

She pushed her cart past the shelves of dog food and cigarettes, then through the automatic door into a flurry of snow. She left Bill a little richer but a lot poorer.

Boo in her pajamas stood on the chair at the dark window, her eyes on the final snowflakes dancing in and out of the street light. The room behind her was a blend of gray and black with shadowy lines scraped upon the ceiling. Harley sat in the dark on their mattress, listening for her father's footsteps, concerned for his safety. It had snowed all afternoon and he was extremely late.

She considered leaving to look for him, but knew that Marci could neither go along nor stay behind alone. All Harley could do was wait. Perhaps if she got Boo to sleep she could sneak out for a moment.

"Do you want a nigh-night song, Boo?"

Boo turned and nodded. "Uh-huh."

"What?"

"*Oh MacDawdle.*"

Harley hated nursery songs with repetitious verses, particularly that one. "How about something else?"

"*Oh MacDawdle.*"

Harley was stuck with farm animals. "All right. But you have to sing, too."

"Oat a."

"*Old MacDonald had a farm, E-I-E-I-O,*" Harley sang alone.

Boo stood on the chair, dipping her knees to the beat and wagging her bottom in four/four time.

"You're supposed to sing with me, Marci."

"Oat a."

Harley started again, still singing by herself. "*Old MacDonald had a farm, F-A-R-M.*" If she had to sing a solo, she would sing it her way. "*And on that farm he had a—*"

Harley paused, waiting for Boo to choose.

"Seep," selected Boo.

"*—a sheep, S-H-E-E-P.*" Harley continued to sing the incessant lyrics using more than *E*s, *I*s and *O*s until she was sick of spelling animals. Their father still was not home.

"Akin!" Boo giggled, demanding an encore.

"No, I'm tired. Let's go to bed."

"Oat a."

Boo climbed off the chair and dived into the blankets before Harley could untuck them.

"You have to say your prayers, Boo."

"Oat a."

Boo rolled out of the covers and knelt on the mattress. Her toes dangled over the edge, nearly touching the floor. She repeated whispers from Harley, twice asking a blessing for their missing father, once for their missing mother.

"Amen," prompted Harley.

"Almond," said Boo as she rolled back under the covers. Harley tucked her in, then sat on her father's mattress to watch Boo slumber.

❧

Jerome walked out of the mall into the cold night. The falling snow had dissipated, but a chilling breeze blew snowdrifts like frozen Sahara sands. The cloudless black sky was dabbled with a billion stars.

Jerome felt snow blow up his Santa pants past his socks to bare knees. He looked left and right along the shoveled sidewalk, then at the two-foot high strip of snow piled along its edge. He either would have to go over the pile or else walk a dozen yards to go around. He decided to challenge the summit. He approached the snow pile and tested its compaction with his boot. It wasn't snowman-making snow, too powdery to support his weight.

He turned perpendicular to the snow strip and hopped sideways over it and the curb, landing one-footed on the ice-packed asphalt. He recognized his stupidity when his boot slipped, but he didn't fall.

The parking lot and cars were blanketed with wind-sculpted snow. In time Jerome found his car among the many, buried bumper to bumper. With his elbow he dusted snow from the door seam, then unpocketed his keys. Slowly, he opened the door, taking care to keep the snow from falling inside, then squeezed his padded body into the driver's seat. Slamming the door, he found himself in a snow cave.

The frigid engine started after some hesitation. He let the engine idle for a minute before turning on the wipers to sweep snow off the windshield. They didn't move. Tiny beads of ice held the blades frozen against the glass. Jerome patted under the seat for the scraper but couldn't find it. He looked in the glove box, then felt under the seat again.

"Great."

He turned the fan switch and slid the lever for air to the windshield, then pressed the button for the rear-window defroster. The fan blew ice-cold air on the windshield. Waiting for the heater to warm up, Jerome rolled his side window down a few inches at a time, pausing often to clear ribbons of snow from the edge as it lowered.

After five minutes of neanderthal efforts to clear snow off the car by mechanical and electrical means, the only cleared window was on the driver's side. The wipers remained frozen in place, and now his breath had frosted the glass inside. Jerome surrendered to the inevitable. He got out, wiped an oval of snow off the windshield and freed the wipers from the grip of ice. The wiper gears immediately engaged, scraping the rubber blades over rock-hard ice droplets splattered across the windshield. After clearing another oval in the rear window, Jerome scurried back into the car and turned off the wipers.

The passenger's side remained caked with snow. His view through the front and back wasn't much better. He turned on the headlights. Snow covering the hood glowed from underneath but didn't illuminate anything beyond the bumper. He clicked on the high beams. The snowy hood glowed brighter.

"Great!"

Jerome got out and kicked snow from his headlights. He got back in and blindly backed out of the parking stall, using his x-ray vision to see through the snow still covering the passenger side, and relying on the good grace of others to compensate for the lack of his own. After backing out without mishap, he made right turns through the parking lot, since he could only see traffic to the left. He was pretty pleased with himself when he made it to the exit with a traffic light where he could make a blind but safe left turn onto the street.

Jerome waited at the red light, his snow-covered rear blinker glowing on and off. When the light turned green he advanced to the middle of the intersection, yielding to oncoming cars. He could no longer see the traffic light dangling above his car, his line of vision obscured by unswiped snow at the top of the windshield. He could, however, tell the signal color by the green ice droplets that glistened like tiny lime gumdrops all over his windshield.

A good head-on would knock the snow off, he thought as he waited to turn. One last car approached the intersection from the opposite direction. The ice droplets changed to yellow. Jerome started his left turn anticipating that the approaching car would stop, but he stomped on the brake as it continued barreling toward the intersection.

Jerome leaned forward to get a direct view of the traffic light. It was still green. He looked for the source of the changed droplet color until the signal really changed to yellow, and made a controlled turn onto the unplowed street, moving to the far right lane.

In a snowy crosswalk ahead, Jerome saw the dark outline of a man with crutches crossing the street, left to right.

"Oh great! The cripple," he said aloud.

The man struggled forward, moving with incrementally small crutch stabs into the mushy snow. It was obvious to Jerome that the light would change before the man would cross. He slowed his car to a slippery stop even though the light was about to change green in his favor. In his rear-view mirror, through the oval, he saw headlights behind him.

Jerome flicked his left signal and tapped his brakes, hoping that those approaching from behind would see his erratic lights and the man with crutches. He panicked as he remembered that his tail lights were covered with snow. To his relief, the truck in the lane beside him slid to a locked-brakes stop just feet from the pedestrian.

The car behind Jerome honked.

"Idiot!" he yelled back. "Can't you see the gimp?"

The man with crutches limped into Jerome's headlights. His fore-head was beaded with sweat. He breathed heavily, snorting steamy wisps that hovered in the light. He had no coat, only doubled sweatshirts. His shoes and lower pants gathered snow as he trudged along, crutches, legs, crutches, legs.

The truck drove through the intersection as soon as its path was clear, splashing a wave of snow onto the man's calves. Other cars drove around Jerome, but he was pinned in place by the pedestrian. The light turned yellow then red as the man stepped beyond Jerome's vision blocked by the snow covering the passenger side.

"He could use some help," Jerome thought, hesitating before reaching toward the passenger door, but as he did the light changed to green. Jerome drove away.

"You're a puke, Jerome."

"Yeah, yeah," he countered, looking in the mirror for the man. Jerome saw no one, but guilt gored his conscience. He pulled over and waited for traffic to clear, then made a fish-tailing U-turn. His headlights brushed across the church lawn, briefly lighting the snow-laden crèche. He drove back to the intersection, sighting the man down the street. There he turned left and slowly drove toward him.

"I don't have time for this," he said, and drove by without stopping.

He forced himself not to look in the mirror, turning right at the next corner. His tire hit the curb, finally jolting enough snow from the passenger side to see through the window. When he circled the block, Jerome found himself back at the mall intersection where he had started, this time from the opposite direction. He noticed a flickering street lamp and concluded that it had been the light source for the non-green gumdrops.

Jerome turned right and again sloshed through the intersection where the man had crossed, looking down the street to his right just in time to see him slip and fall.

"Great!" complained Jerome, wishing he hadn't looked.

He pulled over, checked traffic, fish-tailed another U-turn, ignored the crèche in his headlights, and drove to where the man had fallen.

In his headlights he watched a dark-cloaked raggedy woman scurry across the street to the fallen man. Jerome slowed to watch her hunker down and heft the man to his feet. He was smeared with dirty icy sludge and had to lean on the raggedy woman as they staggered together down the sidewalk.

"Help them," urged a deep thought.

"I'm a puke," admitted Jerome as he drove by.

After his tumble last night, Bill was bruised but not broken anew. His injuries were minor but too painful for the long walk to church, so Harley went alone, leaving Boo with their father.

Harley had insisted on going no matter what. The Junior Sunday School was preparing for the annual holiday pageant, and the girls were assigned roles as shepherds. There were songs to learn and lines to rehearse. Boo could get away with looking cute, a towel draped around her head, but not Harley. She had to be there for practice, and someone had to take care of cleaning the chapel and changing the marquee. It now read:

ONLY TOW MORE SABBATH DAYS TIL CHRISTMAS

Harley closed the marquee and crossed the snow-covered lawn to the crèche. With hands drawn into her coat sleeves, she brushed snow off of the kneeling Mary and Joseph as high as she could, but she wasn't quite tall enough to reach his white-powder yarmulke. She knelt beside the Baby Jesus and wiped snow off the tiny ceramic body. Using her fingernails to clear the delicate crevices of the figurine, she rested her warm palms on the painted skin to melt frozen trickles. With patient effort she cleared all the ice and snow from the nearly naked body before returning to the foyer to hover over the heat vent.

Her numbed fingers and toes still tingled when other parishioners began to arrive, but she abandoned the vent to clean the chapel floors. She found three wrappers, a pink tissue which she tossed in the garbage, and a crumpled cootie catcher which she saved.

The pastor helped Harley wheel the hymnal cases to the chapel doors. She took a book and sat on the front bench where she always wanted to sit but never before could. Sitting in front would require her unfailing reverence.

She didn't fidget during communion.

She didn't yawn.

She didn't wink at Miss Judy the chorister.

She didn't even feel for gum wads under the bench.

When the sermon got boring, she did open her hymn book to add *in the bathtub* to song titles.

After the closing prayer was finally given, the Junior Sunday School stayed in the chapel for practice. Harley let the red-haired teacher know the reason for Marci's absence, then she went to the middle of the bench where her class was supposed to sit.

A strange pudgy boy with oversized ears scooted next to her. Harley reached into her pocket for the cootie catcher, just in case, and politely smiled at him. He grinned back. His broad smile pushed his chunky cheeks into his eyes, making him squint.

"Children," Miss Judy said loudly from the front of the chapel. "Before we begin, we want to welcome two new children to our Sunday School. Eldon and Marvin, will you please stand up?"

The boy next to Harley stood, as did his brother a few benches back. As he stood, the boy grinned bigger than before. His eyes were forced completely shut.

"Thank you, boys. You may be seated."

"What one are you?" Harley whispered as he sat down.

"Marvin," he whispered back. "He's Eldon. I'm Marvin."

"Are you sure?" she teased.

"Yeah. You can ask him if you don't believe me."

"How do I know I can trust him?"

"You can trust him. He's my brother. He'll tell you who I am."

"What will he tell me?"

"That I'm Marvin, and he's Eldon."

"Okay. I'll take his word," Harley snickered.

Miss Judy continued. "Because we have two new children, we need to add a couple parts. Eldon will be another angel, and we'll make Marvin the Christmas star. Marvin, can you come up here, please?"

Marvin stood again, and squeezed past all the knees to the aisle. He walked to the front while Miss Judy explained his part.

"What we'll do, is take the star that we usually hang on the wall up there, and we'll put it on a stick for Marvin to hold way up high."

She showed a broom handle, then held it high to demonstrate the simplicity of the task. She handed the stick to Marvin. He clutched it with both hands, resting one end on the floor.

"No, Marvin. Hold it way up high. Like this," she instructed, motioning upward.

Marvin grinned and squinted, then raised the stick as high as he could.

"That's perfect. Now while we practice, we'll just use the stick. But when it's time for the pageant we'll attach the star to the very top."

"What do I wear?" Marvin asked.

"Some nice church clothes like you've got on now," she answered.

"Can't I wear a costume?"

"You don't need a costume. You are the Christmas star."

"How about I wear a star costume?"

"How about you take your seat, and we'll talk some more after practice?"

Miss Judy took the stick from him and laid it at her feet, then gently pushed Marvin toward his class. He went back to the bench to find that all the girls had scooted to the middle, closing the gap next to Harley. The only spot left was by the teacher.

"All right, children. Remember how we stand together?"

Miss Judy held out her hands, palms down. The children scooted forward to the edge of their seats, except for Marvin who had no idea what was going on. The teacher nudged him forward. Miss Judy circled her hands out, around and up to direct the children to their feet. They all stood in unison except for Marvin who needed another nudge.

"Very good!" complimented Miss Judy. She nodded for the pianist to play an introductory measure, then led the children in song. When they finished, Miss Judy signaled for them to sit.

"Very good! Now, we need Mary and the angel Gabriel to come up for the next song."

Marvin raised his hand.

"Yes, Marvin?"

"Can I be the angel Gabriel?"

"We already have a Gabriel, Marvin. You get to be the star."

"Can I wear an angel costume?"

"Can we please discuss this later, Marvin? Okay?"

"Okay." With no smile on his face and hence no cheek flesh obstructing his eyes, it was easy to see Marvin's disappointment.

The narrator read from the book of St. Luke, then Gabriel and Mary rehearsed their lines. Miss Judy again motioned for the children to stand. They sang and were seated once more.

"You sing so well, children! All right, now let's have Gabriel leave the stage, and Joseph and the Innkeeper come up and join Mary."

Marvin raised his hand. Miss Judy didn't even wait for his question.

"Sorry, Marvin. Tim is playing Joseph."

Marvin inched his hand a little higher.

"No, Marvin. You can't be the Innkeeper."

Marvin dropped his hand.

The scene was rehearsed, and the children sang two more songs.

"I am so impressed! You sing wonderfully!" beamed Miss Judy. "All right. Innkeeper, you may sit down. We need the angels and the shepherds now."

Harley stood and eased her way to the aisle. Marvin had his hand in the air again.

"No, Marvin, we don't need any more shepherds or angels."

He kept his hand high, and stood.

"No, Marvin. You certainly cannot be Mary."

The children all laughed. Marvin danced on tippy-toes, his hand raised even higher. Miss Judy sighed.

"Fine, Marvin. What is it?"

"Isn't the star supposed to be up there now?"

Miss Judy didn't see any harm in adding the star to the current act.

"Okay, Marvin. You may come up."

Marvin strutted to the front of the chapel, nearly blind from his closed-eyed grin. He stood next to Harley and another shepherd.

"Why don't you come over here by me, Marvin?" Miss Judy suggested. "This is a good place for the star."

Marvin walked to Miss Judy and stood with his back to the congregation.

"Always face the audience," she whispered while rotating him.

"Can I hold the stick?" he asked.

"Sure, why not?"

Miss Judy raised her hands out, palms down. The seated children shifted forward, ready to stand.

Marvin bent over to pick up the stick at her feet.

Miss Judy circled her hands out, around and up.

The children stood.

Marvin picked up the stick, snagging it under Miss Judy's dress. He hefted the stick high above his head, raising her dress inside-out above her head like a flag, but no one pledged allegiance. Instead, the young congregation burst into uncontrolled laughter at the sight of her intimate apparel.

Miss Judy screamed and slapped at the lifted dress. Marvin stood proudly with the stick held high, grinning with squinted eyes, unable to see anything. The pianist dodged around angels to save Miss Judy, but Harley beat her to the rescue. She yanked the stick from Marvin, retiring the colors and freeing the chorister. Harley held the stick away from Marvin, denying his efforts to regain possession, as Miss Judy dashed from the chapel screaming.

After a long break and an exchange of roles, the new shepherd Marvin stood far, far away from Miss Judy's place.

❦

Fully dressed for the afternoon shift, Jerome drove by the church on his way to the mall. He appreciated the tip that there were only "tow" more Sabbath days until Christmas.

"Doofs," he jeered, scratching his upper lip through the beard.

He stopped at the traffic light just up the street from where he had abandoned the man with the crutches. He peered down the street, half expecting to see him and the raggedy woman still struggling along the sidewalk. In the distance he saw a girl in a hooded pink coat.

Harley, he thought, *walking the streets alone again. Her parents should be shot.*

Jerome glanced at the car clock, then compared it to his watch. There was time to kill before his shift. When the light changed he looked over his shoulder to make sure no cars were behind him, then made a wide-left turn from the far-right lane.

Santa slowly approached the pink-coated girl from behind. He was sure it was Harley. He tried to keep a distance, but his car coasted faster than she walked. When she unexpectedly stopped to gaze into a pet store window, Jerome scanned the curb ahead for open parking. He parallel parked just past the pet store and waited with the engine running. Harley soon turned from the window and started walking his direction.

Dressed as Santa, Jerome was as covert as a teenage boy in a lingerie shop. He quickly considered his alternatives for hiding. Pressing his face against the passenger seat and squishing his foam padding as flat as possible, he lay there contorted, his feet near the brake, his hips under the steering wheel, and his head buried in a mass of white hair on the seat.

He pictured Harley in his mind, calculating the amount of time it would take for her to pass by. He then added a countdown of ten extra seconds for good measure. When he reached blastoff, he pushed up from his contorted position.

Harley stood next to his car, staring at him through the passenger window. She rolled her eyes and shook her head before walking away.

"That was good," Jerome said.

He waited until she was half a block away before he started to follow again. Harley never looked back. Two blocks from the pet store, she turned a corner to her right, and disappeared from his view around a building.

Jerome signaled to follow her until he saw the large DO NOT ENTER and ONE WAY signs. He stopped half-turned into the intersection to look up the street. Harley was now up the block walking backward. She laughed, waved, and stuck out her tongue, then turned to continue up the one-way street.

Jerome jammed his car into reverse and parked by a hydrant. He shut off the engine and ran up the sidewalk after Harley, bouncing along in fur and velvet. He watched her enter a small neighborhood grocery store on the corner ahead, apparently unaware that the cat-and-mouse chase was still on.

As soon as Harley stepped into the store and out of Santa's view, she hurried to the back and stepped through the double-hinged doors marked EMPLOYEES ONLY. She stopped them from swinging and peeked between the gap. The moment Santa stepped into the store, she slipped out the side door and was gone.

Jerome moseyed through the small maze of aisles searching for Harley, eventually dead-ending at a shelf filled with personal hygiene products. He smelled spice. Suddenly he knew why Harley annoyed him so. Her smart-aleck attitude reminded him of the instigator, that sixth-grade girl who ruined his career by initiating *the incident*. Not one administrator sided with him in spite of his vehement denials of liability, and the fact that the school district and his insurer paid nuisance settlements only fueled the flame of scrutiny among his fellow teachers.

Unlike the instigator, Harley would not prevail.

Jerome saw Moreen and Scotty down the corridor. He lifted the toddler from his lap and stood at attention with child in arms to announce the arrival of Prince Snotty.

The photographer elf tittered. Santa retook his seat just as Moreen stepped on the porch. She heard the cackling but ignored it.

"When you're finished with this one, we need to talk," she advised, frost in her voice.

"I'm done now," Jerome answered, shooing the toddler away.

He followed Moreen behind the North Pole to the men's rest room.

"See if it's occupied," she ordered.

He pushed through the door and looked under each stall.

"All clear," he yelled.

As Moreen stepped inside, Jerome flushed an empty toilet to startle her.

"You didn't want to see that," he said.

"Thank you. That was thoughtful."

"You're welcome. What's up?"

"I have your paycheck here. I wanted to explain it to you before I left."

"You're leaving us?"

"I'm going *home*. You know, Jerome, you could show more respect."

You're in the men's room, and you want respect? he thought. "What about my paycheck?" he asked.

Moreen cleared her throat for a speech. "Jerome, you are a valued employee. You have been good for us, and we have been good for you. However, this mosquito fiasco merits a lesson to be learned. Accordingly, I've docked your paycheck fifty dollars."

"You docked fifty dollars for what?"

"I docked fifty dollars for the cost of mosquito abatement. Mr. Ludwig has had to squeegee mosquito eggs every afternoon. His time costs us money. You brought the mosquitoes in, it's only fair that you pay to get the mosquitoes out."

"What kind of bull drool has the janitor been feeding you? I had nothing to do with any mosquitoes!"

"No one fed me anything, Jerome. You confessed last week about the mothballs. If it weren't for Mr. Ludwig, the Health Department would have shut us down. You should count your lucky stars we stayed open for business, or your negligence would have cost a small fortune! Be glad it's only fifty dollars. If you don't like it, you can always walk."

Profanities perched on Jerome's tongue like starlings on a wire. He was about to let them fly when the rest room door swung open. A little boy pranced in, knees together. His eyes got big when he saw Santa, and even bigger when he saw Moreen.

"It's okay, young man. We were just leaving," said Moreen.

"I'll be right out," Jerome said through gritted teeth. He rested on the counter until the boy finished and left. Three minutes later, a less angry Santa emerged from a less clean rest room.

Jerome returned to Santa's porch where Scotty waited at the head of the line. "Hello, Prince. Did you get that adoption mess figured out?"

"Yeah, I guess. Mom said the boys didn't know what they were talking about."

"Have your friends ever told you anything about me?"

"Like what?"

"Oh, I don't know. Next time you see your friends, ask them if they believe in Old Saint Nick. Then ask your mommy what she thinks. Okay?"

"Okay."

"Have you decided what to get your mother for Christmas?"

"No."

"Before you do, come talk to me and we'll decide on the perfect gift. Something special, just for her. Something she *really* deserves. Like mothballs, or spice perfume. Okay?"

"Okay."

"Good. Anything else?"

"Nope."

"Great. Be good and be gone." Jerome lifted Scotty by his back belt loop to give him a wedgy. He noticed Harley and Boo by the fountain, saying good-byes to the janitor, and thought about further revenge against Mr. Ludwig. Nothing outstandingly devious came to mind. Perhaps an opportunity would present itself through the girls. He could hardly wait to talk to them.

"Hello, Boo," he said when they got to the front of the short line.

"Harrow, Sand Clods," she said, climbing onto his lap.

"Hello, Harley. Long time no see."

"My name is not Harley, and you saw me yesterday."

"Was that you? I'm sorry. I should have offered you a ride. But you wouldn't take a ride from a stranger, would you?"

"Especially weird ones," she answered.

Jerome ignored the insult, conniving a way to get even with the janitor. "You must know Mr. Ludwig pretty well. Is he your friend?"

"So what if he is?" said Harley.

"Nothing. Just curious. How long have you known him?"

"Long enough."

"Doesn't your mom care about strangers giving you money?"

"He doesn't give us money. He lets us take it."

"Now there's a distinction without a difference," Jerome responded. "Okay. Doesn't your mom care about strangers letting you *take* money?"

Harley didn't have an answer. Jerome went on.

"You know, you could get into big trouble. There are people here who do horrible things to children that take money from the fountain."

"You mean like Moron and Wiener," Harley commented.

Jerome smiled. "Yes. Like Moron and Wiener. Do they know the janitor lets you take money?"

"Maybe."

"Or maybe not."

"Sometimes they watch us."

"Moron and Wiener watch you take money?"

"They watch us pretend to kill mosquitoes."

"Did the janitor lie about mosquitoes to keep you from getting in trouble?"

Harley's conscience was cornered. "I guess, maybe. He was just joshing."

Jerome felt a twinge of remorse for venting his spleen in the rest room. Still, he wanted to recoup the docked fifty dollars.

"So. What are you going to get with your money?"

"Stuff for Boo."

"Like what?"

"I don't know."

"Maybe you could get her a picture with Santa."

Harley made a face. "I don't think so."

Jerome re-situated Boo on his knee to see her face. "All right, Boo, your turn. Tell me what you want for Christmas. Slowly." He put his hand on her small shoulder and paid his best attention.

"Eye needle tofu Hurry's buff tie."

"Maybe your sister can help," he said, looking to Harley. She licked her teeth as she shook her head *no*.

He turned back to Boo. "I really don't know what you want, Boo. Can you show me somehow? Can you color me a present?"

She smiled and reached into her partly zipped coat to pull out Baby Bear. She held it to Jerome's nose, and spoke very slowly.

"Hurry cave Mossy Bevy Bayer foamy booth tie. Eye needle tofu Hurry's buffed egg."

Santa turned back to Harley. "Boo wants a new Baby Bear? Is that it?"

Harley answered out of shear frustration.

"She doesn't want a Baby Bear. That's not what she said. She's just saying that I gave her Baby Bear for her birthday."

"Oh. Okay. Thanks." He returned his attention to Boo. "So Harley gave you Baby Bear. Now, what do you want from Santa Claus?"

Boo laid Baby Bear on her lap. She placed her small hands against Santa's beard, just under his cheeks, and pulled his face close to hers.

"Mossy wands a pleasant fur Hurry."

Jerome really tried, but still only heard illogical mix-matched words. "I'm sorry, Boo, but I'm not getting this. Your sister has to help."

"Well, Santa, her sister isn't going to help," Harley interrupted. "We have to go."

Jerome confirmed the late afternoon hour on his watch. "Are you coming back tomorrow?"

"We might come after school, if you promise not to call me Harley."

"You got it, Princess," he agreed.

"Or Princess."

"No problemo, Rump," he answered with a wink. "Make me a picture, Boo," he said as he gave them each a candy cane. On their way down the corridor the girls waved to Mr. Ludwig as he wheeled a bucket and mop into the men's rest room.

Jerome slowed his car to get a better look. The sight on the church lawn made him titter so much that fibers of the curly mustache tickled his nose, giving him a sneeze sensation. Some hooligan had stolen a plastic pink flamingo and placed it in the crèche beside the Holy Family.

"Now that's rich," he snickered, admiring the handiwork of the late-night artiste.

He was still smiling as he cruised the mall lot to find good parking. Ahead he saw Moreen exit through a service door with keys in one hand and a large shopping bag in the other. She hustled to her car across the icy asphalt lane, sidestepping snow puddles on the way. It appeared she might get into her car and vacate the prime parking space.

Jerome stopped a few car lengths away to let her back out, but she simply opened the trunk and tossed the bag inside, then hurried back into the mall without even looking in Jerome's direction.

"Bummer," he said, driving forward to renew his search for good parking.

When he passed Moreen's car, he saw that it was parked in a stall reserved for the physically challenged.

"This parking fiasco merits a lesson to be learned," he mocked, parroting the words Moreen had used to dock his pay.

He double parked to inspect the tag hanging from her rear-view mirror, confirming his suspicions. "Totally fake!" he sneered, raising his fists and dancing to the *Theme from Rocky* in his mind.

He jogged to the service entrance and called mall security from the wall telephone.

A raspy male voice answered. "Security."

Jerome pinched his nostrils. "Yes. Good afternoon," he whined. "Get me Mr. Charles."

"Speaking."

"This is Werner Hilledge. I'm calling to see if you value your job."

"Yes, Mr. Hilledge. Of course I do."

"Then you won't mind doing it, will you? I have just seen another illegally parked car. I believe it is *your* job, not mine, to patrol the parking area to curb such lawlessness. I want you off your keester and on your feet, patrolling the mall and doing your job. And get that car towed away post haste, do you hear me?"

"Yes, sir. I'll get on it right away!"

Jerome fully described Moreen's car and its location, then reminded Mr. Charles that his job was on the line. He raced back to his car and drove away just as Mr. Charles emerged from the service door.

Jerome parked where he could get a good view of the impending action. Soon three more security officers were hovering around Moreen's car, walkie talkies against their mouths. Within ten minutes a tow truck arrived.

As Moreen's car was hitched for towing, a very jolly Santa sauntered into the mall.

✂✿✄

The mid-week afternoon saw a lull in shopping activity. No one was in line to see Santa, so Jerome stood to circulate the blood in his thighs.

"Ho ho hum!" he said to the elf. "You want to yawn some carols?"

"Sounds like fun," the elf answered.

"Well, you have a good time," Jerome replied, leaving the elf to head for the fountain.

The janitor and the girls had their backs to him as he quietly approached. When within a yard of them, he pinched his nose and spoke.

"What on earth are you doing with my money, Mr. Ludwig!?"

The janitor and Harley whirled around with expressions of guilty shock, followed by disgusted relief. Jerome let go of his nose and bellowed with laughter. "Gotcha!"

"Very funny," scoffed Mr. Ludwig.

"Yeah, very funny," Harley concurred.

"Berry funky," mimicked Boo.

"So, how's the fishing today?" Jerome asked. "Can I see your license?"

"Berry funky," said Mr. Ludwig. "When did you become a game warden?"

"When do you become an exterminator? I'm out fifty bucks because of your mosquito story."

"So I heard. Moron wanted more, but I talked her down to fifty."

"Well, *that* was nice of you. You couldn't talk her down to zero?"

"I tried, but she wanted to tattoo your—" The janitor paused and looked at the little ears present, then cleared his throat. "Your *whazoo*. You became the scapegoat for Skeeter-gate. So I owe you fifty bucks."

"Tell you what," Jerome responded. "After Christmas, get my fifty from the fountain. Give me twenty-five, and you keep twenty-five."

"There you go. We'll be partners in crime," said the janitor. "I'll repay your fifty without tapping the fountain."

"No. You don't understand. I don't want *you* to pay anything. The mall owes me the money. You get half for your inconvenience."

"My inconvenience?"

"Well, yeah. You know. The clogged toilets. I heard some guy did a number on them yesterday. You didn't deserve the inconvenience."

"Is that a confession?"

"It's a vicarious confession from the guy that did it."

The janitor grimaced to suppress a smile. "Did this guy also number one the walls?"

"No! I only did a number with paper towels. No other numbers were involved."

Mr. Ludwig laughed at the remorseful Santa.

"So, we split the fifty?" Jerome asked again.

The janitor relented. "We'll split fifty. After Christmas."

Jerome looked at the North Pole. There was still no one in line, but he thought he should get back before Moreen came along.

Santa stooped to talk to Boo. "Do you want to visit Santa here or over at the big chair?"

Boo shrugged her shoulders.

"Here," said Harley.

"Then here it is." Jerome sat on the fountain rim and placed Boo on his knee. "Okay. Let's pick up where we left off yesterday. You're still a good girl, right?"

Boo nodded.

"I thought so. Now, what do you want for Christmas, very slowly."

Boo cleared her small throat, then swallowed. "Police tan eye half sum fling fur Hurry."

Boo's request was again met with a blank stare from Santa, but Mr. Ludwig bent forward to assist.

"No, pumpkin. Tell Santa what *you* want for Christmas."

She redirected her request to Mr. Ludwig. "Boo watts a tofu Hurries buffed egg."

A stymied Santa sat in awe as Boo and the janitor engaged in small talk.

"But isn't there something *you* want?" asked Mr. Ludwig.

Boo shook her head. "Hurry gamy Bevy Bayer. Huh knees a Chrysalis peasant foe huh buff dye."

"Wouldn't you like a dolly or something?"

"No. Eye waddle tofu Hurry."

Mr. Ludwig was thoroughly amazed. Jerome was thoroughly confused.

"What does she want?" Santa begged to know. "Tell me."

"No, don't," instructed Harley. "Don't tell him anything. She doesn't need anything from him, especially that."

"Especially what?!" Jerome pleaded. "Doesn't Santa get a say in what she gets for Christmas?"

"No," responded Harley.

"I guess not," observed Mr. Ludwig.

"Kiss snot," said Boo.

❧◌◦◌❧

Santa Claus lounged on the throne with no visitors. He stared straight ahead, not focused on anything in particular, listening to the canned Christmas music over the PA and wishing he could understand Boo lingo. So far, the only substantive thing he had understood was Harley's name.

A rancid voice interrupted his thoughts.

"Jerome," beckoned Moreen.

He awoke from his mid-shift dream and rolled his eyes toward her. "Some crowd, eh?" he answered.

"I need a ride home. My car's in the shop."

Jerome perked up. He hadn't considered this consequence. "You want me to see who's going your way?"

"No, Jerome. I need you to give me a ride home."

Great! he thought. "Great," he said. "Where will you be when it's time to go?"

"Right here. It's time to go."

"But I still have two hours before closing. Who's going to greet the kids?"

Moreen glared at him, then at the empty lines. "You'll be missed like a cold sore, Santa. Take me home, and if you want you can come back."

Jerome sought an appeal. "Have you cleared this with Werner? I don't want him thinking I left early."

"Werner isn't here. He's on a cruise."

"On a cruise? Since when?"

"Since Friday."

Jerome swallowed hard. The gulp was audible through his thick beard. It wouldn't take Scotland Yard long to figure out that somebody other than Werner had called on her car.

"A cruise? Does his wife know?"

"Yuck, yuck," jeered Moreen. "Let's go."

Jerome went directly to the janitor's closet, carrying his Santa outfit in a bundle. He rapped on the locked door.

"What?" yelled Mr. Ludwig from inside.

"Little pig, little pig, let me in," said Jerome.

"Wise guy," answered the janitor as he swung open the door. He held a half-eaten sandwich in his hand. "Well, what is it?" he asked.

"Smells like tuna."

"Wise guy. What is it that you want?"

"Information about the girls."

"What for?"

"So I can get to know them."

"What for?"

"For my community service hours. You know what for."

"So you can help them?"

"Right."

"Why?"

"Why? Because they need it."

Mr. Ludwig took another bite of sandwich. "All right," he finally said. "What do you need to know?"

"For starters, do you know their names?"

"Yes."

Jerome waited for an answer. It didn't come. "Well, what are they?"

"Girls," jabbed the janitor.

"No. What are their names?"

"Harley and Boo."

"What about their last name?"

"How would I know?"

"They didn't tell you their last name?"

"They didn't tell me their *first* names. You did."

"You got their names from me?"

"Yes. Who else would I get them from?"

"From them."

"Why would they tell me their names? I'm a stranger."

Jerome rubbed his fingers on his forehead, and scratched the side of his nose. "Could you ask about their last name and where they live?"

"What for?"

"So I can help."

"Aren't you taking this a little too personal? The girls need help, but what makes you think you're the man?"

"What makes you think I'm not?"

"Because you don't *really* care."

"And you're the only one who does?"

"No. Truth is, I don't really care either."

"*You* don't care? Give me a stinking break."

"I didn't say I didn't care. I said I don't *really* care."

"Right. You don't give a damn."

The janitor shrugged. "Giving damns is easy. Giving more is tough. I personally haven't given anything. I won't let it get personal. If you do, you get a guilt complex. You can't solve the problems of every kid that comes to the mall."

Jerome couldn't believe what he was hearing. "Oh, *please*. I've seen you with them."

"Any fool can watch little girls bob for money. It's like watching a guy eat from a dumpster. What am I going to do, go buy him some ketchup? I couldn't begin to solve the world's problems. Neither can you."

"Unreal."

"Oh no, it's real. You know and I know that whatever you might do is a drop in the bucket. It's all relatively futile. So tell me, Santa man. You really think you can make a difference? *You* get real. The only reason you're here is because Harley has you pegged as a phony. Am I right?"

Jerome hated that the janitor saw through him so easily. "So what if I am? Just tell me what Boo wants for Christmas."

"She wants the same thing Harley wants: something to give. Boo wants something for Harley."

"What?"

"I don't know," answered Mr. Ludwig. "And I don't think I want to know."

꒰◔◡◔꒱

Santa sat in the throne, watching the girls and the janitor. Every so often the janitor looked over, then quickly away. If not for their earlier discussion, Jerome never would have thought Mr. Ludwig to be emotionally aloof.

After looting the fountain, the girls came to Santa's porch. Boo was singing *Shingle Pails.*

"Hello, Boo," Jerome greeted, lifting her up.

"Harrow, Sand Clocks."

"Hello Harley. Have you both been good?"

Boo nodded. Harley did not.

"So, Boo. Tell me what you want for Christmas."

"Iguana pleasant foe Hurry."

"And why do you want a present for Harley?" he asked while looking for Harley's reaction to his newly acquired gift of tongues. She pursed her lips.

"Mossy needle tofu Hurry's buffed egg."

Jerome understood the part about needing a toy for Harley, but that was it. "What kind of toy?"

Boo shrugged.

"Does she need a Baby Bear like yours?"

Boo shook her head. "Hurry cave me Bevy Bayer."

"Harley gave you Baby Bear?"

She nodded.

"Who gave Baby Bear to Harley?"

"Mama."

"Where's your mama?"

"That's enough," said Harley. "You've asked her enough."

Jerome wanted more, but backed off from the interview. "Thank you, Boo," he said, giving her a cane. He reached for Harley. "Come here a minute."

She shook her head but didn't resist his gentle tug. Jerome put his arm on her shoulder and spoke softly. "Will you tell me what you want for Christmas?"

"No."

"Please?"

She shook her head.

"Will you tell me what Boo wants for herself?"

"No."

"Are you still mad at me for missing your house last year?"

She reflected on the question. "No. We moved. Maybe we were too hard to find."

"Maybe. Will you help me find you this year?"

Harley stared back at him before wiggling from under his arm.

"No. We need to go."

Jerome handed Harley a cluster of candy canes.

"Tuck these in your coat. Hang them on your tree." He immediately wished he could retract the words. They wouldn't have a tree if they couldn't afford gifts. "Do you want a picture with Santa? For free?"

"No thanks," answered Harley as she backed away.

"Snow fangs," affirmed Boo.

Day Sixteen, Thursday

After stepping off the bus, Harley paused to zip her coat before chuffing along the sidewalk, her chin in the air, breathing blasts of steam in and out of her nose like a choo-choo train. Clouded air rolled over her forehead as she chugged toward the church. When she felt more than air flowing through her nose, she lowered her head to wipe the drip.

Harley stopped in her tracks. Santa was parked at the curb in front of the church a few yards ahead. Was he waiting for her? There was no escape from his view.

She dreaded eye contact with him but looked his direction anyway, prepared to stare him down. He wasn't even looking her way. He was laughing at the Nativity scene on the church lawn. Then he rotated to look over his left shoulder and accelerated his car into a traffic gap.

Harley stood like a deer in headlights until she remembered her father's tales about sneaking into movies by walking backward against exiting crowds. She spun her backside to Santa's car and walked in reverse step.

Jerome hardly noticed the girl on the sidewalk, recognizing her as Harley only after glancing in the mirror. He didn't have time to stop.

Harley continued walking backward even after the tail lights of Santa's car were out of sight. She exhaled puffs of steam as she chuffed across the church lawn, stopping at the crèche to remove a plastic gnome set by the Baby Jesus. She laid it in the trash on a bed of souring half-pint milk cartons before going inside to get Marci.

❧❀❧

"Hello, Harley. Hello, Boo," Santa greeted.
"Mister Claus," Harley said.
"Mustard Claws," said Boo.
Jerome felt nosy. "I saw you walking by yourself to the mall."
"I saw you laughing at Jesus."
"You saw wrong."
"So did you."

"Where was Boo?"

"Someplace."

"Someplace where?"

"Someplace else."

"Did she walk here by herself?"

"No, *duh*. She's too little."

"I know she is, *duh*," he answered, miffed. "How did she get here? Did your mom dump her off?"

"No. She got here with me."

"Did you stop by your house?"

"No. My house is too far away, *duh*."

Jerome had had it with the duhs. "You better tell me how Boo got here."

"Or what? You won't bring me anything for Christmas? Woo-hoo."

"Woo-hoo nothing. Boo shouldn't be roaming the streets. It's criminal."

"It's also none of your business."

"I'm making it my business. I won't let you and your irresponsible parents ruin her life."

Jerome lifted Boo onto his knee to initiate another investigation. "Boo, did you walk here by yourself?"

Boo shook her head.

"See, I told you, you big fat jerk!" said Harley. "You don't listen."

"I am not a big fat jerk. This is padding. And I don't listen because you don't say anything worth listening to. If you said something worth listening to, maybe I could make things better."

Harley stepped forward to confront Santa. "How could you make things better!?"

"First off, get your mom and dad here and I'll make them better parents!"

Harley gritted her teeth, her eyes churning a storm.

Against better judgment, Jerome sighted the cross-hairs of his scope on her heart. "Where's your mom, Princess?"

Harley inched her scowling face closer to Santa's.

"Where's your dad?" Jerome bulldozed. "Is he a drunk? Does he like the booze? Or maybe he's a crack head."

Jerome saw fury rising on Harley's face. He drew back an inch, fearing an immediate head-butt, or beard-yank, or shin-kick.

Boo squeezed her small body between them.

"Tatty," Boo informed Santa, "half ass dent."

Hearing individual words but missing their collective meaning, Jerome burst into laughter.

Harley cocked her fist and pummeled Santa with a punch to the nose. Pain crossed the bridge to his forehead. A spangle of stars obscured his vision, one star glowing brighter than all. Cheers and claps erupted from the crowd. *Deck the Halls* played on the sound system. Jerome heard Harley screaming above the din.

"You are so stupid! She said daddy had an accident!"

Once again, Jerome sat humiliated with all eyes on him, except those of the elf who had turned his back.

Harley shivered and inhaled, but no tears escaped her welling eyes. Jerome didn't know what to say, but he spoke anyway. "Is he in the hospital?"

"No," she answered with a rattle in her voice.

"Is he all right?"

Harley shook her head *no*.

"What's the matter with him?"

When Harley said nothing, Boo spoke up.

"Tatty bloke hiss lakes."

"Does he have crutches?"

Boo nodded.

"Was he hurt on a motorcycle?" Jerome asked.

Harley responded with a mixed expression of anger and disbelief. "No," she answered.

"Does he like motorcycles?"

"No, *duh*."

"Then why did he name you Harley?"

She closed her eyes and held them shut. "You are *so* dumb. He did not name me Harley." She grabbed Boo by the elbow and pulled her away. "Let's go, Boo. Say bye bye to Santa Clod."

"Bubble, Sandal Clog," said Boo. "Sea ewe a morrow."

"No you won't," Harley corrected.

"Parting is such sweet sorrow," scoffed Jerome as he waved them away. *Just like the instigator,* he thought as he looked around for Moreen.

Trrue to her word, Harley did not take Boo to the mall after school. Instead, the girls stopped to look at puppies in the pet shop window. Boo couldn't see very well, so Harley hefted her up on a hip. Boo pressed her forehead against the pane to watch two puppies nip and wrestle. A third puppy slumbered in a mound of shredded newspaper.

"Luck," said Boo pressing her pointy finger against the glass. "Poop."

Harley giggled at the observation, so much that she almost dropped Boo. She set Boo down and laughed until her sides hurt. It took her a few minutes to stop.

"Come on, let's go home," she snickered.

"Poop," said Boo, making her laugh again. They staggered down the sidewalk giggling, warmed by the juvenile humor.

"Tan eye half sum canny?" Boo asked as they approached the street that led up to the corner store.

"We have candy canes at home."

"*Police* tan eye half sum canny?"

Harley looked at Boo and then at the store up the street. She had one quarter in her pocket. "All right. But I get to choose."

As the girls entered the store, they saw a young mother at the counter holding a snugly wrapped baby. Another child about Boo's size fidgeted near his mother. He had no coat, only a tattered sweater. Broken laces knotted his shoes. His socks were two different colors. His cheeks were chill chaffed, and his nose dripped yellow green.

"Luck, Hurry, p—" Boo started to say.

"Quiet," scolded Harley, putting her hand over Boo's mouth. "That's enough."

The owner spoke to the woman. "Let's call it even."

"No. Here." She removed a can from the nearly empty bag and handed it to him. He looked at the price, and credited the amount with a few keystrokes on the cash register.

"Seven eighty-seven," he said.

"This should do it," she said, handing him another can. He stroked the register again.

"Seven forty-one."

Stacks of change lay on the counter. The woman picked up three coins before the owner scooped the others into the register drawer. He closed it with a clang.

The pockets on the woman's fleece jacket were frayed and holey. She dropped the three coins into the bag and bent over to pick up her son. With a child in each arm, she nabbed the bag with both hands and hugged her three bundles close. Boo held the door open as the woman stepped into the cold street. Harley grabbed a taffy stick and slapped it on the counter with her quarter.

Boo started to protest. "No. Eye—"

"Too bad," said Harley. "It's this or nothing."

She handed Boo the taffy, got her change and pulled Boo outside. Instead of crossing the street toward home, they followed the woman up the street a few blocks where she entered an old building through a weathered wooden door.

Harley and Boo rushed to the building door, opening it just enough to peek inside. They watched the woman climb the first flight of stairs before slipping inside.

Harley listened to the woman's tired feet skid against stair treads, and to her labored breaths. The girls tip-toed up the first flight, then the second, stopping when the woman spoke.

"I've got to put you down, Skyler." His feet hit the floor, then a key pushed into a lock.

"Wait here," Harley whispered to Boo. "Don't move."

Harley climbed a few steps to look through the stair banister to see the boy, the woman's legs, and the small bag of groceries at their feet.

"Hurry," whispered Boo.

Harley glared down the steps, holding a finger to her lips.

The apartment door creaked open. The boy scampered inside.

"Hurry," Boo whispered again.

Harley glared again and mouthed a shut up.

"Poop," said Boo loudly.

Harley snorted, blowing a snot bubble as she jumped down the steps laughing.

"Run!" she hooted as she took Boo's hand on the fly.

The girls ran down the stairs and banged through the wooden door, resting against the building only long enough to catch their breath. They retraced their steps down the street before cutting through the park to go home.

After a supper of radiator-heated soup and bread, the girls yipped, nipped and wrestled until they were dog tired. When darkness conquered the apartment, they rolled onto their mattress panting.

"Do you want a story, Boo?"

Marci grinned and nodded.

"What story?"

"Chrysalis," she answered.

"Again?"

Boo nodded.

"Okay, if that's what you want." Harley made herself comfortable. "When Baby Jesus was born, He didn't have any place to live. There was no room for them at the inn, so the innkeeper let them live in a manger with horses and cows. Did you know that Jesus didn't have a nice bed like us?"

Boo nodded.

"Jesus had to sleep on hay. Would you like to sleep on hay outside?"

"Nuh-uh."

"Me neither. When Jesus was born, angels sang songs because they were so happy. And shepherds saw the angels, and they were sure afraid. But the angels said 'fear not,' so the shepherds stopped being afraid. Are you going to be a shepherd at church?"

Boo nodded and ran to the bathroom to pull her blue towel off the bar. Harley wrapped it around Boo's head as a shepherd's turban, holding it in back since she didn't have a clothespin.

"How's that?"

"Awl white."

"Good. Now, if you saw an angel, would you be sure afraid?"

Boo shook her head *no*. It wig-wagged inside the loose-fitting towel.

"Neither would I. The angels told the shepherds where the Baby Jesus was. So they went and they kneeled down. And there was a star in the sky and three kings followed it. Do you know where the star took them?"

Boo nodded.

"Where?"

"Two Cheeses."

"That's right. And they gave Him gold, frankincense, and myrrh. Do you think Jesus liked that?"

"Uh-huh."

"Should we look for the star?"

Boo nodded and jumped up, leaving the towel in Harley's hand to climb onto the chair by the window. Harley knelt on the chair beside her.

"There's a lot of stars out there, huh?"

Boo nodded.

"Which one do you think is *the* star?"

Boo tapped her fingernail against the glass, pointing to a small, bright star low on the horizon.

"Me, too. I think that's the one."

Harley thought about the woman and her two children, unable to get them off her mind.

"Boo. Tomorrow should we pretend we're kings and go visit the Baby Jesus?"

"Yeah!" Boo clapped. "Well bee kinks foe Cheeses!"

⁓⦿⁓

Jerome stood at his bedroom window, listening to his wife brush her teeth. The beautiful clear night was illuminated by moonlight gleaming off the undisturbed snow crystals that blanketed his back lawn.

Sure beats mowing, he thought, knowing that he skated on winter chores. His wife always shoveled the driveway and walks because he was gone most every evening. She had even winterized their inherited rental home by herself.

Jerome glanced from star to star to see if any might be satellites. One star on the horizon caught his attention. It flickered a pulsating glow, but didn't move like a satellite. He thought about the girls and wondered if they would ever come back to the mall.

"What are you looking at?" his wife asked as she emerged from the bathroom.

"Nothing, really. Just looking and thinking."

"About what?"

Jerome never really discussed things with his wife. They talked but rarely conversed. He didn't discuss his work or his dreams. She knew he hated teaching, just not how much. Jerome had never even told her about the girls, and right now he wasn't in the mood. What would he tell her, anyway?

"Not much," he answered.

"Ready for bed?"

Jerome wondered what it would be like to have children of his own, but dismissed the question as moot. Fathering a child was impossible given his sluggish glands. What if he swallowed his pride and consented to adoption? Could he be a good father?

"Not quite," he answered.

"Want a back rub?"

Jerome surveyed his large back yard with its smooth untouched blanket of snow. It had no swing set, no tree house, no sand box. He had never raked leaves for pile diving. He had never filled an inflatable pool. No snow fort was ever built, no baseball ever thrown in that yard.

"Is there a catch?" he asked.

Day Eighteen, Saturday

The low hum of the refrigerator motor rattled through the house, keeping Jerome awake. He couldn't stop thinking about Harley and Boo. The dawn eked through the vertical blinds and taffeta drapes, casting jail bars of dim blue light across the vaulted ceiling. Cozily buried under thick blankets and a down comforter, he stared at the odd-shaped shadow patterns above him.

Jerome could no longer ignore the usual morning discomforts. His hair was matted, his mouth was filmy and his bladder was full. He rolled over to look at the clock radio. It was barely after six.

"Go find the girls," he thought. "Stay in bed," he muttered aloud.

"Pick up your teeth," his sleeping wife rambled, "I just mopped the car."

"Eye needle piddle," Jerome answered as he slipped from bed.

❦

Jerome drove past the pet store and the park, then around the block to access the one-way street with the corner store. He cruised by the store riding the brake, tipping up his sunglasses for a clear look through the front door. His view was partly obscured by the OPEN sign hanging from a suction cup, but he saw a girl in a pink coat.

"Bingo!" he giggled as he parked by a NO PARKING sign. He strutted across the street, zipping his leather flight jacket and adjusting his sunglasses. His car and clothes revealed a relative wealth unusual to the neighborhood.

Through the window he saw Harley and Boo at the counter.

Sometimes I amaze myself, he thought.

A bell on a chain banged against the door as it opened. The owner and Harley looked up, then went back to business. Boo continued to make fingerprints on the counter's glass front, too occupied to look up.

"Morning," said Jerome using his Werner voice.

"Yup," replied the owner.

"Where's the deodorant?"

The owner pointed to the back corner.

That was smooth, Jerome muttered in his mind. *Where's the deodorant?*

He went to the back aisle and pretended to compare antiperspirants, holding them side by side to read ingredients. He soon became engrossed in the hygienic wonders of aluminum hydrates.

The cash register chimed with repeated keystrokes followed by sounds of cans loaded into plastic bags. With a final beep and a whir from the register, the owner announced the total.

"Forty-four twenty-one."

Harley hefted a scarred milk carton onto the counter and dumped its contents into a pile.

"You gotta be kidding. Doesn't anyone carry bills?" The owner then mildly scolded Boo. "And stop it with the fingers on the glass!"

Boo looked at Harley for a second opinion and received an evil eye.

"No more, Boo. Hands off."

"Oat a."

The owner counted coins while Harley watched for sleight of hand maneuvers. Boo wandered to the aisle where Jerome stood. He waved, then went back to reading deodorants. Boo stared at the dark reflective lenses on his bespectacled face as she flapped her arms. Then she stopped and cocked her head to one side.

"Luck, Hurry," she said pointing up the aisle. "Sand Claws."

Jerome stepped back in total surprise, bumping into a life-size cardboard cutout and knocking it off its base. He turned to steady the cutout and noticed its caricature for the first time. He smiled.

Harley left the counter to look up the aisle. She saw some man steadying a cardboard Santa who was spraying his underarms.

"Yeah, that's Santa Claus. Now stay with me," she scolded, pulling Boo back to the counter.

"You got thirty-five dollars and sixty cents," the owner said. "We need to put a few things back."

Jerome considered stepping forward to correct the owner's grammar and to drop a bill on the counter, but he decided to wait and follow the girls home. The owner pulled cans from the plastic bags and keystroked credits, not bothering to ask what Harley wanted to keep. She didn't complain until he pulled baby food jars.

"Not those. Something else," she instructed.

With Harley's attention diverted, Boo again wandered to Santa's aisle. Jerome put his hand under the cutout's armpit and waved. She waved back.

"Get over here, Boo, or that stranger will get you," threatened Harley.

Boo smiled, giving a two-handed clam-wave before returning to the counter.

"Okay," said the owner, "we're at thirty-seven sixty-eight. Let's call it even."

"Thank you very much," said Harley.

"Dang shoe berry mulch."

Jerome heard crinkling bags and the clang of the chained bell.

"Cow pie, Sandy Clogs," yelled Boo as the door closed with a thud.

The owner walked from behind the counter and looked up the aisle. "Are you gonna buy something? This ain't a library, you know."

"I seem to have forgotten my wallet. I'll be right back," fibbed Jerome as he rushed by the owner out the door. The girls were up the sidewalk to his right. The owner watched from the store window as Jerome crossed the street to make his pursuit less obvious. He lagged behind, stooping often to tie his shoes. When the girls entered an old building, he crossed the street and followed them inside.

He paused in the foyer, listening to their small feet shuffle up the stairs, and counted the number of flights they climbed. Then he heard a knock. A creaking door opened, and a muffled voice spoke from three flights up.

"Skyler, close the door! I'll be out in a minute."

Harley's distant voice was next. "Here, Skyler. Help me put this stuff on the table."

The door creaked closed. Jerome ran up the stairs and listened at apartment doors until he heard Harley's voice. He was tempted to knock and announce himself, but he opted to make a grand full-handed entrance. He returned to the street below, giddy as a foal.

This will show Miss Smartypants, he laughed, jogging back to the corner store. He grabbed a basket and strolled the aisles to select foodstuff from the limited stock. When he set a full basket on the counter, he looked at the candy display and chose a Mr. Goodbar.

"Breakfast," he said putting the chocolate in the basket. "How much for the cardboard Santa?"

"It ain't on sale."

"It ain't *for* sale," Jerome corrected, "but everything has its price. You saw how much the little girl liked it."

"If it's for the girl, she can have it. For you, it's ten bucks."

"It's for the girl. She lives just up the street, you know," he said thumbing over his shoulder.

The owner rang up the purchases. "Sixty dollars forty-three cents."

Jerome opened his wallet and extracted three of his five twenties, tossing them on the counter. "Call it even?" he asked.

"No." The owner removed the Mr. Goodbar from a bag.

"Not that," said Jerome. "Something else."

The owner swapped the chocolate bar for two cans, and credited the amount. "Sixty dollars even."

Jerome peered over his sunglasses, questioning the amount.

"Sixty dollars," confirmed the owner, slapping the bills into the register.

Jerome nabbed the bags and headed for the street. He stopped with his hand on the door. "Oh yeah. The Santa," he said as he returned to the back corner. He wedged the cutout under his arm and left the store.

Hike or drive, he contemplated as he stepped over the threshold. *Drive,* he decided, crossing to his car. He maneuvered the cardboard Santa into the passenger seat and stuffed the groceries under it, then drove away, devouring the candy bar even before circling the block. He parked in front of the old building and gathered his delivery, humming a carol and singing the lyrics in his mind.

Good King Wence-slas
Went to town,
Ri-ding on a po-ny.

Bags in hand and cutout underarm, Jerome climbed the stairs and rapped on the door. Skyler opened it. His mother rushed to the door.

"Skyler!" she scolded. "I told you don't open the door!"

"It's okay," said Jerome. "I'm a friend of Harley and Boo."

"Wrong apartment." She pushed on the door, but Jerome put his foot in the way.

"Right apartment. I saw them come home. I even see the groceries on the table."

The woman pushed harder. "Two girls brought me stuff, but they don't live here."

"Right. If they don't live here, where do they live?"

"I have no idea. They just showed up, talking about the Wise Men and Baby Jesus. Then they left."

"When?"

"Just now."

"Which way did they go?"

"Which way do you go when you leave a building?" she answered.

Jerome took his foot from the door. It slammed closed. He ran down the stairs, thumping the cardboard Santa on the steps and banging the bags of canned goods against his knees. The girls were no where to be seen. He stood on the sidewalk until his fingers hurt from holding the bags.

"You may as well give the food to the lady," he thought.

"Maybe I can get my money back."

"When pigs fly. Leave the food!"

Jerome threw the Santa cutout in the foyer and again ascended the stairs. He set the bags by the apartment door, knocked, and returned to his car empty handed. He circled the block twice, but after finding no trace of Harley and Boo he went home to make trails in his backyard snow.

Harley stood over the vent, letting her pants absorb the blowing heat. Boo roamed the church foyer, squatting to pick at specks in the carpet, then stomping them like bugs. The church was otherwise empty and quiet, awaiting the arrival of its parishioners.

"Go watch Daddy," said Harley in an effort to stop Boo from stomping.

"Oat a," Boo replied.

She went to the entrance door and leaned her cheek against the glass to watch her father arrange letters on the marquee. Snowflakes fluttered around him, some resting on his head and shoulders.

Boo's eyes and mouth opened wide. She pressed her pointy finger against the glass and gasped. "Luck, Hurry! Sam Cloths!"

Harley scurried to the door. She cupped her hands around her eyes and squinted to see through the fogging pane. She also gasped.

Santa was parked at the curb, yelling at her father. She couldn't hear what was said, but knowing him as she did it had to be profane.

"Excuse me," Jerome yelled through the open passenger window to the man with crutches.

Bill turned from the sign. "Hey, Santa! Lose your sleigh?" he joked, crutching toward the curb.

Harley's pulse quickened. Her thoughts went wild. Her father was going to get in Santa's car.

"No, dad, no!" she screamed. "He's a stranger!"

Bill heard a faint screech behind him, like the distant meow of a cat getting its tail yanked.

"What's up?" he asked Santa, leaning into the car window.

"Do you live around here?" Jerome inquired.

"Not quite, but I know the area. What are you looking for?"

"Well, I wondered if you were acquainted with a Harley."

"As in a motorcycle?"

"As in a kid."

"A kid? Named Harley?"

"Yes."

Bill stuck his head deeper into Santa's window. There was another cat yowl. "You got me. Sorry," he said.

Jerome's intuition had failed. He had thought for sure this man was Harley's father. "Do you know a Fanny Withers around here?"

Bill shook his head. "Nope. Sorry again."

"Well, it does," snickered Santa.

Bill smiled. "It's been a while since I heard that one."

Jerome noticed the lawn crèche had a new decoration. Next to Mary a yellow daisy pinwheel spun in the cold breeze. "Nice job on the manger," he remarked. "Who's your decorator?"

"Oh, that. It happens every year. Some fool trying to be funny."

"It *is* pretty amusing."

"Not when you think about it."

Jerome thought about it. "No, I guess it isn't. I'll let you get back to your sign. Thanks."

Bill stepped away from the car. "Anytime. Merry Christmas."

"And to you," said Jerome, noticing the sign. It read:

ONLY ONE MORE SABBATH DAY TIL CHRISTMAS

Jerome yelled again to the man with crutches. "By the way, you spelled *TIL* wrong. It should be T-I-L-L. *Until* only has one L, but *till* has two."

"You're right. It does. Thanks," Bill answered, resting his hand on the car hood.

Another muffled scream came from the church foyer.

"Sounds like your church mouse is killing a cat," said Santa as he drove from the curb.

Day Twenty, Monday

anta sat on his throne, pleased to see Harley and Boo waiting at the fountain for Mr. Ludwig. He was somewhat surprised they had come back to the mall, though he doubted they would come to see him later. It was probably better that they stay away, since Harley had a way of raising his dander.

Three children and two parents waited in line to see Santa. For some inexplicable reason Jerome now spent more time with each kid. Although he wouldn't admit it, he was starting to enjoy the childish discussions.

He didn't even notice Moreen approach with her son. She butted Scotty to the front of the very short line and left to go about mall business. Jerome took his sweet time with the child on his lap, until the brat stepped forward.

"I haven't got all day, Santa," Scotty said, sounding like his mother.

Jerome covered the ears of the child on his lap. "Get off my porch, and get to the back of the line where you belong."

Scotty listened in disbelief. "Do you know who I am?"

"Yes," answered Santa with a grunt, his hands still over the child's ears. "And I know where you live, and I know what you want, and I'll flush your presents down the toilet if you don't get off my porch and back to the back of the line. Now git."

Scotty's jaw dropped. He didn't move until he got a follow-up glare, then he went to the back of the line, but stayed only long enough to survey the area for his mother. When he couldn't find her, he left the line to sit on a bench by the fountain a few paces from Harley and Boo.

The two parents in line gave Santa four thumbs up, as the *Hallelujah* chorus played on the sound system.

Jerome returned his attention to the child on his knee, discussing cartoons and trikes, comics and room cleaning. He heard a sudden ruckus.

"Mama! Mama!" screamed Scotty. "Help me!"

Jerome looked up to see the taller, older Scotty holding Harley by the wrist, tugging at her fist clenched full of coins. She struggled and pulled, but couldn't get free of his grasp. Mr. Ludwig was nowhere in sight.

"Mama! She's taking all your money!"

Jerome looked down the corridor beyond the fountain and saw

Moreen peering around a Roman column. She scowled, lifted her skirt and stomped up the corridor toward the fountain.

"Oh great!" exclaimed Jerome.

He scooted the child off his lap, hurdled a velvet rope from the porch, and ran toward Harley and Scotty, but Moreen already had chugged her hefty body around the fountain to the melee. She grabbed Harley's arm above Scotty's wrist hold. Harley yanked and writhed to get loose, her eyes glazed with panic.

"What's going on here!?" Moreen demanded.

Jerome arrived. "I've got her! I've got her!" he proclaimed, nabbing Harley's elbow with one hand and Scotty's arm with the other. He twisted and yanked Harley's wrist free from Scotty's grasp. Coins flew from her fist and chinked on the floor as Jerome wedged himself into the group and butted Scotty away.

One down, one to go, thought Jerome. "I've got her! I've got her!" he repeated as he peeled away Moreen's fingers, ramming her with his hip. She screamed and toppled sideways, her waist landing on the fountain rim, her outstretched arm and hair splashing into the water. She teeter-tottered on the rim, head over pond and feet over floor.

"I've got her! I've got her!" Jerome announced to the gathering crowd. He winked at a terrified Harley and freed his hold. "Stop! Thief!" he yelled as she ran to Boo.

He pretended to give chase and slip, kneeing Moreen's extended legs to make her a human spin-the-bottle. She twirled off the rim onto the floor, landing on her stomach with a sloppy thump and mopping the tile with her hair.

Harley and Boo had escaped.

"Are you all right?" Jerome asked, bending over Moreen.

"Get the girl!" she yelled.

"Tally ho!"

Jerome lunged to the edge of the crowd and hopped up and down, pretending to look for Harley. He zigzagged through people, looking around bodies and between legs. During his feigned effort he found Harley's pink coat on the bench. His heart sank. He ran back to Moreen, her back against the fountain sitting in a puddle. Mascara trickled down her face like clown tears. She had never looked more lovely.

"I found her coat," he reported. "Now I'll find her."

"Bring her to me."

"Yes ma'am."

Jerome ran down the corridor to the outside door. Light snow dusted the sidewalk. He saw small footprints but couldn't see the girls anywhere. He followed the prints around a corner of the building where a blast of frosty wind whipped the cap off his head. He chased it, stomped it, picked it up and packed it in his coat pocket, then draped Harley's coat over his head to cover his wig.

The wind had cleared the sidewalk on the side of the building. Jerome ran ahead without a trail to follow. The star on the black horizon caught his attention.

"Keep going. You'll find them," he thought, but the cold wind made him consider other options. He decided to get his car, and re-entered the mall for a warmer route to where it was parked.

"Jerome!" he heard a repulsive voice yell as he sneaked past the North Pole. At the photo counter, a soggy Moreen stood with Scotty and Mr. Charles from security. She smelled of wet dog.

"Where's the girl?" she asked.

"I'm still looking. I'm checking all the exits."

"No. You're done. Get back to work."

"But we can catch them if we hurry."

"*Them?* What do you mean *them?*" Moreen demanded.

"*Her.* We could catch her."

Moreen scowled through her smeared makeup. "Do you know this girl, Jerome?"

"No. I mean I've seen her when she came to see Santa, that's about it."

"That's about it, what?"

"That's about it, *nada.* That's it."

"What is her name?"

"Rumpelstiltskin. How should I know?"

"You don't know her name?"

Jerome swallowed. "No." He knew she knew he knew.

"Get back to work, Jerome. You're done. Mr. Charles will take it from here."

Jerome turned to step away.

"Aren't you forgetting something, Jerome?" Moreen held out her hand, but he faked confusion. She continued. "The coat. Give me the coat."

Now his heart really sank. Jerome hesitated but still gave it up. With a single motion, Moreen snatched the coat and gave it to Mr. Charles. He looked inside the collar.

"Just what I thought," he said. "Her name and address are right here."

Jerome couldn't believe it. He cowered to his throne. The thought of Harley without her coat sickened him. He sat there nauseated, watching Moreen and Mr. Charles search through Harley's coat pockets, putting coins they found into Scotty's hand.

As soon as Moreen and Scotty left for home, Jerome had the elf close the North Pole. Santa had some shopping to do.

⚬⚬⚬

Jerome drummed his fingers on the large sack on the passenger seat as he drove down the one-way street toward the corner store. The thick falling snow was now sticking to the road. The sign on the door was turned to OPEN. He parked at the curb, shut off the wipers and headlights, and grabbed the sack. Locking the car door as it swung open, he kicked it shut and bounded across the dark street. The owner turned the sign to CLOSED and inserted a key in the deadbolt just as he got to the door. Jerome pushed the door open before the owner could turn the key.

"Get lost, Santa. I'm closed. I don't need no last minute robbery."

"I'm not here to rob you. I need help."

"Then see a shrink. I'm closed." The owner pushed on the door. Santa pushed back.

"Wait. I need *your* help. I have coats for some girls you know."

The owner stopped resisting and let Santa in. "I swear, mister, if you rob me I will hunt you down and stick my foot so far—"

"Now stop it. I said I'm not going to rob you." Jerome tugged the beard below his chin to reveal his face. "I was here on Saturday with two little girls that bought some food. And then I bought some food and that Santa spraying gunk in his armpit. I need to know where the girls live."

The owner looked at him carefully. "You was the guy with shades?"

"*Were.* I were—was the guy with shades."

The owner muttered a profanity. "I knew you was staking me out!" He stepped behind the counter, opened the cash register and began to throw bills into a bag for Jerome.

"Enough with the money. I was not staking you out."

The owner stopped. He stared at Jerome, still unsure. "You said you was giving the Santa thing to the girls. You said they live up the street. How come now you say you don't know where they live?" He started to put bills into the bag again.

"Because I followed them to the wrong place. I thought I knew where they lived, but I didn't."

"So you didn't give them the cardboard thing?"

"No."

"Then you owe me twenty bucks."

"You said ten on Saturday."

"Inflation. I want my twenty bucks."

"I'm not paying twenty for that piece of junk."

The owner stooped behind the counter and stood with a bat. "You ain't leaving till you pay."

"So now *you're* going to rob *me*? I don't think so." Jerome put his hand into the pocket of his Santa jacket and formed a finger gun. "Drop the bat!"

The owner looked at the pocketed weapon. He giggled and set the bat on the counter, then mockingly put his hands in the air. Jerome looked down at his finger weapon and joined in the laughter.

"Look," said Jerome. "I'll give you twenty if you tell me where the girls live."

"Keep your twenty. I don't know."

"Don't they come here often?"

"They come here enough. I see them maybe once a week."

"So if I leave something, could you give it to them? I bought them coats."

The owner thought for a moment. "Leave the coats and your number. I'll give them to the girls next time they come in."

"You give me your word?"

"My word."

"Fair enough. Got a pen?"

Jerome wrote his phone number on the sack, then the owner stuffed it under the counter. They left the store together. Jerome stopped under the eaves with his back to the wall to watch the dense snow clusters quietly fall to the street. The owner rolled the protective iron covers over the windows and door, and clipped each with a padlock. He then said good-bye to Santa and walked to his car parked on the side street.

Jerome stayed where he was, absorbing the moment. He could see no sky through the thick snow, but his thoughts were on the hidden stars.

He felt like he could walk on water as he crossed the empty dark street. He patted his pockets. The keys! Adrenaline shot through his body. Jerome checked the door to verify he was locked out, then wiped snow off the window to see the key still in the ignition. He circled the car to check each door, then rushed back to the store. The owner's footprints led to deep tire tracks of a now gone automobile.

Jerome looked around the building. There was no pay phone. He walked down the slippery sidewalk to the next corner and looked for an open business. The poorly lit street was quiet and abandoned. He looked at his watch. It was 10:40. Snow was piling atop his wig, and his hands were getting cold.

He looked at his car. He could break a window.

He looked back at the store. He could not break a window.

He looked at the mall lights in the distance. He could walk the six blocks and catch a late bus.

He looked at the apartment buildings on the far side of the park. He could knock on doors until he found a friendly face.

Under a street lamp near one building he saw a pay phone. He looked again at the long walk to the mall and decided to call his wife.

Jerome took note of the street sign so he could give good directions before blazing a diagonal path through the snow-blanketed park. He shook the gathering flakes off his shoulders and stomped his feet when he arrived at the phone, wiping the icy phone receiver on his jacket. He pressed it against his ear under the wig. No dial tone. He pressed O. No response. He pressed 911. He inspected the phone and wiggled the wires, but couldn't get it to work.

"To the mall," he proclaimed half aloud, and returned to the path he had just blazed through the park. His feet scrunched the fresh snow on the frozen grass underneath. The pleasant sound echoed off nearby trees, reverberating louder and louder as he approached a glade. The echoing seemed louder than it should be. He stopped.

The scrunching continued.

Jerome took off in a dead run, burdened by foam padding that suddenly felt like lead. He slipped and slid, barely staying upright. The scrunching from behind got closer and closer. He prayed to get to the street, hoping that a motorist would happen by.

A hand grabbed his jacket and yanked him back. Jerome slid to one knee, but came up swinging. The wig dropped over his eyes, blindfolding him with a mass of hair. He kicked and punched misdirected blows at the unseen foe who pummeled him with callused knuckles in the face. The Santa beard scraped across his eyes like steel wool. Behind the grunts of his assailant there was more scrunching snow. Others were joining the ambush.

Jerome yelled for help, but only once. He took a swing kick to the knee. His feet flew from under him. He felt a hand on his beard. With a forceful tug, the beard's ribbon reached its maximum elasticity, tearing at his ear. As the beard came off his head, Jerome cupped his ear to press away the pain. He felt the flow of hot blood in his palm.

The assailant raised Santa's hair high over head and howled a savage yell. "You've been scalped, old man!"

Jerome staggered to his feet, huffing shallow breaths of clouded air, an exhausted bull facing a toreador. He glanced around to see how many others were there. Two stood behind the toreador, waiting for a command.

The toreador grinned a sinister smile, then spit in Jerome's face.

"You're a puke," Jerome retorted, wiping his face with his sleeve.

A hand slapped his bleeding ear. Jerome cradled his head in his elbows and dropped to his knees in a fetal position, burrowing his arms and head into the deep snow. He felt blows to his ribs, and was grateful for the padding. He took a brutal stomp to his hip.

"Wait!" shouted the toreador. "You're messing up the suit. Get it off first!"

Jerome felt them tug at his jacket. He reached under his chest and yanked at the buttons and belt, praying for amnesty once they had it off. His arms were jerked back as the jacket was yanked away.

"Now!" yelled the toreador.

Jerome again wrapped his arms around his head. His arm and chin were pelted with blows. His jaw popped, his ears rang. He took repeated hits to his chest. The foam now felt like gauze.

Jerome knew he wouldn't survive if he stayed on the ground.

He sprang to his feet and charged, ramming his forehead into the toreador's nose. Both fell to the ground, Jerome on top. He pummeled the toreador's face until a kick landed against his shoulder blade. Like a child throwing a tantrum, he kicked the toreador's head until the others pulled their leader away. Jerome rolled to his knees, disoriented and in extreme pain, too weak to stand.

He could no longer defend himself when the two returned. They thrashed him until the toreador raised his hand.

"Stop! He's mine."

The assault halted. The sound of the toreador's approaching feet was deafening. Jerome teetered on a cliff of consciousness as they rolled him over, eyes up. He sensed scalding cold moisture over his body, a mixture of blood, sweat and snow.

He couldn't focus his vision, seeing only blurred gray images. He tasted blood and phlegm on his tongue. The salty mass drooled from his mouth. Jerome gasped for breath and felt the chilling sting of a cracked tooth. Greater pain centered in his chest. With each breath it rippled to his extremities.

The toreador paced over him.

"Do him!" encouraged one assailant, his voice as from a tunnel.

Warm steel pressed heavily against Jerome's cheek.

"In the head? Or in the heart?" asked the toreador.

Jerome heard the metallic click of a pistol hammer engaged to fire. He wished for complete unconsciousness, willing to end this nightmare by fading to black. His thoughts dimmed. A distant match light flickered in the cavern of his mind.

"Help is on the way," whispered a voice from within. Jerome began to weep, consoled by the promise of deliverance, whatever its source might be.

"Merry Christmas, Santa," declared the toreador.

Jerome heard the thunder of rapid-fire popping as the flickering light went dark. He surrendered his soul to God.

Day Twenty-One, Tuesday

The squad car's flashing lights lit the neighborhood with a throbbing crimson glow. The rookie behind the wheel shined his spotlight on the rear license plate of the illegally parked car. He radioed the number to dispatch, then waited for a response.

"You have a possible stolen vehicle," dispatch reported. "There's a missing-persons report on the owner, called in about two hours ago."

The rookie checked the time. 3:20 a.m. "What time was that report of gunfire in the area?"

"22:45."

"Then I better look to see if anyone is toes up in the car."

"Ten four."

The rookie grabbed his khaki wool coat and tugged it on, then opened the glove box to get his metal flashlight. He reached under the dash and popped the trunk latch. Stepping from the warm car, he hustled to the trunk and shined the weak flashlight inside, shaking it to joggle the batteries. He squinted to find the snowbrush with the dim light.

He approached the parked car, looking around to assure his personal safety. The driver's door was locked. The rookie whisked snow off the window, and aimed the dim flashlight inside, then brushed snow from the adjacent window to check the back seat before returning to his squad car.

He held the transmitter to his mouth. "Nobody, and *no body*, is in the car, but the key is in the ignition. Looks like he locked himself out."

"Any evidence of foul play?"

"Not anymore. Just snow. I'll look around."

"Ten four."

The rookie coasted the squad car past the abandoned vehicle, scanning his spotlight across the snow-pelted park. Near the center he spotted a suspicious snowy mound. Again he contacted dispatch.

"I see something in the park. Could be our missing person. I'm going to check it out."

"Ten four. You need homicide?"

"Hope not. You'll be the first to know."

"Ten four."

He locked the spotlight on the mound, its brightness piercing the rhythm of red overhead lights. He left his car and trudged toward the mound.

Harley awoke, troubled by a bad dream. Her heart beat in syncopation with a throbbing glow from the window. She lay completely still to listen for signs of life around her. Boo's warm body and her father's rattled breathing dispelled her fear of being alone.

The flashing red light invited her to come and see. Quietly, she slipped from the blankets and crept to the window, pushing aside the cardboard. She saw a police officer cutting a deep snow trail across the park. A spotlight behind him etched his elongated shadow across the alternating white and red snow. She watched him crouch beside a mound in the middle of the park.

The rookie sat on his haunches, hesitating to touch anything. He had never investigated a homicide before, and didn't want to compromise any evidence. The thought of a frozen body sickened him in spite of all the autopsy photos he had seen at the academy.

He shined the dim flashlight over the mound. The snow-covered body lay in a near fetal position. With a trembling finger he cleared a spoon-sized circle at the head to verify what was underneath. The lifeless surface felt like slimy cold plastic to his careful touch. He held the weak light closer to see what he had cleared. A large swollen eyeball stared back at him.

The rookie fell backward off his heels and scooted from the mound before jumping to his feet and racing toward the spotlight on his car. Nausea overcame him as he ran. He bent to vomit, and heaved the contents of his stomach in a steaming pool at his feet. Using fresh snow, he moved to rinse his mouth, but stopped before his contaminated fingers could reach his lips. Instead, he scrubbed his hands.

After radioing for homicide, he cordoned the perimeter of the park with yellow barricade tape. It took at least twenty minutes for a detective to arrive.

"I secured the area when I confirmed there was a homicide," the rookie advised.

"First murder?" asked the detective, reaching into his coat pocket.

The rookie nodded.

"Next time swallow harder," scoffed the detective, handing him a roll of Lifesavers. "Where's the stiff?"

"Under that pile of snow. I made sure to not disturb him."

"*Disturb* him? A dead guy?" The detective laughed as he ducked under the tape. The rookie followed.

"No, you wait here. Keep the area secure," the detective said. "Let's not disturb the stiff anymore than we have to."

He walked to the mound and stood over it, shining his bright flashlight on the eyeball. He used the toe of his shoe to scrape snow off the head, laughing at what he uncovered.

The stiff's face was chestnut brown. His lips were stretched tight against his teeth in a surrealistic smile. His enlarged nose was cherry red. Antler-like fragments protruded from his head.

"Say cheese, Rudolph," giggled the detective as he took a Polaroid. He kicked more snow off the nude shoulders, laughing at the rigid figure, then yelled to the rookie. "Hey, Rookie. You want to give me a hand here with Rudolph?"

The rookie scowled. He ducked under the tape and walked to the mound, angry. As he drew near, the detective shined the flashlight in his face, making him shield his eyes with a forearm.

"It's tradition to take a photo of a cop and his first murder," said the detective. "Lie down."

"You make me sick," answered the blinded rookie. "This is going in my report."

"Can't wait to read it. *Everybody* should get a load of this. Now lie down before I tag this buck and strap it to your bumper!"

The rookie stared at the uncovered mound, his pupils re-dilating. He blinked in disbelief as his eyes focused on the lifeless carcass of a hollow plastic deer.

There had been no body under the snow. His first homicide was a large leaping lawn ornament, an infamous red-nosed reindeer.

⚬⚬⚬

Jerome floated on turbulent black clouds churning across a dark moonless sky. Blood-red stallions appeared from nowhere, trampling his rigored body under hoof, then stampeding at the sight of a black-winged angel. She first offered comfort by stroking Jerome's forehead, then she and other fearsome beings dragged him to a hellish tomb of fire and smoke.

The dream of horses and demons played over and again like a bad movie on cable until the faint scent of ammonia made Jerome aware of his continued existence. He tried to awaken, but his eyelids were too heavy, his body too thick. It felt like diluted Novocain flowed through his tingling veins.

Exerting all his strength, Jerome lifted his head to verify his mortality. Synapses responded by zapping pain through his numb limbs. He lowered his head and lay still until the pain ripples ceased. He tried to evaluate his condition without moving.

A constant high-pitched tone rang in a scabbing ear encrusted with hair. The touch of his tongue against a cracked tooth made him wince. His spine felt like a collection of clam shells, and his hip was tenderized chuck.

Jerome sensed no catheter, no IV, no oxygen line. He sniffed again to smell the ammonia. It had a non-clinical aroma.

For what seemed hours he drifted between sense and sleep until a pinstream of light pushed through a tiny knothole in a boarded window. The beam rested on his brow, nicking his eyelid. As he inched his head from the light, he sensed the presence of others in the dark, dank room. He now recognized the ammonia smell. Urine.

He blinked to clear his vision. A raggedy woman stood watch over him. Her torn clothes and tattered black shawl gave her a winged angelic appearance.

"How ya feelin'?" she asked.

Jerome opened his mouth to speak. His jaw ached. "Like death warmed over," he answered through tight lips.

"Well, you don' look *that* good, but you're alive."

Jerome tried to absorb more of his surroundings. Dust floated in and out of the sunlight sneaking through slats nailed over windows. The ceiling was tarnished with soot. He heard crackling embers from a fire barrel. Floorboards creaked as people walked. The room reeked of smoke, excrement, and body odor. He longed for spice.

He tried again to sit up. Cold air crept under the blanket.

"Where are my pants?" he groaned.

"They's here." The raggedy woman pointed to a crate used as a table.

"My coat?"

She smiled and winked.

"Those boys won that tug-a-war. But I won me the Kewpie doll."

Her wide gaping smile was wonderful. He returned a smile even though it hurt. He thought about his favorite holiday shirt with the mistletoe.

"My shirt . . . and the foam?"

"Your shirt was all bloody, so we throwed it in the fire. Luis there took the foam for a pillow. I told him to leave it be, but he said you was gonna die anyhow."

Jerome looked to the opposite wall to see a filthy creature perched atop Santa's padding. Stubble covered the man's head, and a clumpy beard grew from his chin. Grime and dirt were caked on his skin, particularly his hands, obscuring his ethnicity. Elephantine wrinkles dug deep into his forehead, a stark contrast to the woman's smooth complexion.

Jerome considered all the microorganisms trekking from Luis to the virgin foam frontier beneath him.

"Luis can have the padding," he said, "even if I live."

"You hear that, Luis? He says you can have it."

Luis mumbled something unintelligible.

"He says thank you," she interpreted.

"I say he's welcome," Jerome said as he closed his eyes.

He remembered his dream and the ambush in the park. A rush of fear made him close his eyes to squeeze back tears. The woman must have seen Jerome's anxiety.

"Don't you worry 'bout nothin'. We took care of them boys. They're long gone. And you still got all your parts. I seen that everything is still there."

Jerome opened his eyes to see a teasing smile. He felt his face flush.

"Don' worry 'bout it," she laughed. "I got boys your age."

Jerome sighed, calmed by her voice. "Did you kill them?"

"My boys?"

"No, the guys in the park."

"No. Nobody killed nobody."

"I heard gunfire."

"No. You heard wood."

Jerome's wincing eyes expressed his confusion. In answer to his unspoken query, the woman walked to a woodpile and got two scrap boards. She slapped them together rapidly, rifling loud pops that sounded like gunfire. She tossed the boards in the barrel, and waved the embers with a plastic plate to kindle a flame.

"Them boys must a been vampires. They sure was scared of wood," she said through her wonderful smile.

It was time for a formal introduction. "My name is Jerome. Thank you." Water trickled from his eye to his ear.

"I'm Annie. It wasn't nothing. You just rest."

Annie tucked the blanket around Jerome's shoulders. He closed his eyes, listening to the now pleasant popping of the wood fire.

"When I saw the fire last night," he whispered, "I thought I was in hell."

"No. This ain't hell. I've been there."

"Where?"

Annie paused before answering. "Hell—and heaven both—was when I had a home. My boys made it heaven. My man made it hell."

Like Annie, Jerome supposed his home was heaven. As for hell, anywhere with Moreen remained high on his list, but the park now topped it.

"You hungry?" asked Annie.

He indicated *no* with a slight move of his head. "It hurts to chew. I could use a drink."

"Soda okay? I got me some in my bag."

"Sounds good."

Annie dragged a duffel across the room, then dug through it until she found a half-consumed bottle of cola with a pop-top cap. She knelt, and helped Jerome raise his head to sip. The cola chilled his cracked tooth, making him pull back. Cola dribbled down his neck.

"Ooo, that's cold."

"Here, let me get you somethin' to put on." Annie walked to a box near Luis and pawed through it. He growled at her.

"Pipe down, Luis. The man lived, so you got to make a fair trade. That's the way it is." She removed a checkered summer-weight shirt from Luis's box and returned to Jerome. "Here. Luis says you can have this."

Jerome peeked around Annie. Luis glared back.

"Are you sure?"

"Yeah, or he gots to give you back the foam."

"I don't want the foam. I really don't. Thank you Luis."

Annie carefully slipped the shirt onto Jerome. The pain from moving his limbs made him grit his teeth.

"Can you hand me my pants, please?" he asked when the shirt was on. Jerome tried to slip the pants under the blanket to maneuver his feet into the legs.

"You need help?"

"No. I can get it."

"You want help getting up?"

"No. I think I'll try this sitting down."

Jerome fussed with the pants a while longer.

"Should I turn my back so you can stand up?" Annie asked.

He nodded. She smiled and turned slightly, keeping one eye on him. Jerome struggled to his feet, swaying from dizziness. Annie stepped forward to steady his stance. She helped him put each leg in, and tugged the over-sized suspenders onto his shoulders. Without padding around his torso the large red trousers sagged below his hips. He gathered the excess material into a bunch.

"I could use a belt," he said.

"I got tape. Think you can stand by yourself?"

He teetered as she rummaged through her duffel bag, emerging with a roll of duct tape.

"I found this in the trash," she said. "A dog chewed it."

Pockmarks from canine teeth perforated the tape, keeping her from pulling a long strip without it tearing. She bit, tore and pasted bits of tape around the waist of Jerome's pants until they were snug.

He stood there dizzy, St. Nick in a checkered-shirt cocoon. Annie draped a blanket on his shoulders and helped him rotate on his bare feet to get a panoramic view of the room and its occupants as she introduced him to the fearsome beings of his dream.

"You met Luis. Luis, this is Jerome."

Jerome nodded. Luis moaned and looked away.

"Jerome, this is Rat. Rat, Jerome."

A man stepped from a dark corner of the room into the dingy light, his hand extended.

"Rat?" questioned Jerome.

"Rat," Annie affirmed.

"How do you do, Rat?"

"Good. And you?" answered Rat. The extended hand hadn't touched soap in the recent past. Jerome shook it anyway, but wiped his hand on his pants when Rat walked into the hall.

"And that's Ike, still asleep," Annie continued, pointing to the backside of a man in khaki curled in a ball on the floor. He had no blanket, and used his forearm for a pillow.

"I am *not* asleep," Ike responded without moving.

"Nice to meet you," said Jerome.

"And that's Ike's friend, Elijah," Annie said, pointing at an empty chair. She whispered into Jerome's ear. "Don't never sit on Elijah."

Jerome nodded. He didn't want to offend a crazed veteran.

Ike stretched out of his curled position. "Elijah is *not* in the chair. Do you see Elijah? Don't tell people that Elijah is in the chair unless you see him in the chair."

Jerome saw an opportunity to befriend Ike. "May I sit in the chair to put my boots on?" he asked.

"No, you may not sit in the chair. Are you deaf *and* dumb? She just told you that is Elijah's chair. Nobody but Elijah sits there. What if he showed up while you were lolligagging in his chair?"

Jerome knew about Elijah's hoped-for visits during Passover, but that was three months away. "May I just sit on one side, so if Elijah comes he'll still have half a chair? I'll be out before Passover."

"One more time. This is Elijah's chair. It's not just for Passover. Elijah is welcome here anytime. Nobody but Elijah sits in the chair."

Annie gave an I-told-you-so look to Jerome.

"I apologize," said Jerome. "I won't ask again."

"Apology accepted," said Ike. "You'll have to sit someplace else."

Ike left the room, and returned with an empty bucket. He set it upside down by Jerome, then he and Annie helped him sit.

Annie felt inside Jerome's boots.

"Luis? Did you take this man's socks?"

Luis grumbled a denial, but Ike walked over and patted him down. He found the stockings under his arms.

There was a sudden crash in the hall, followed by frantic stomping of heavy feet. Jerome stiffened, jolting pain through his body. No one else reacted.

With a loud stomp, the ruckus ceased as suddenly as it began. Rat entered from the hall, proudly pinching a large freshly killed rodent by the tail. He whirled it around his head like a lasso, then heaved it into the fire barrel. After nodding victoriously around the room, he returned to the hall.

"That's why we call him Rat," said Annie.

⁂

Annie led the way as Ike and Rat hauled Jerome to the corner store using the boy-scout chair carry. Luis walked caboose, mumbling.

The store owner called 911, then opened a bottle of rubbing alcohol and a package of pads to cleanse Jerome's superficial wounds. Within minutes the rookie arrived. The black-winged angel and her hellish entourage retreated to the park after loading Jerome into the squad car.

Jerome was too sore and exhausted to ask about the plastic deer in the back seat. He silently thanked God for his strange deliverance, hugging the soiled blanket that Annie had left with him.

Boo in her pink coat and Harley in a sweater watched from the corner as the police car sped by. Boo waved at Santa, but he was too sleepy to wave back.

✄◯◯✄

Mr. Charles sat in his white police-surplus car, comparing the address on the coat label with the house number painted on the porch step. He got out and walked along the chain-link fence, scoffing at the BEWARE OF DOG sign. Harley's pink coat bunched in his hand, he stopped at the gate to look and listen. No fence separated the back yard from the front. He saw no yellow snow, no piles, no paw prints, no evidence of a dog. The sign was a ruse.

Mr. Charles opened the gate and strutted to the front porch of the gray shingled house. Ignoring the doorbell, he knocked on the metal edge of the storm door, then knocked again. The dead bolt of the inner door clicked and opened only as far as the safety chain permitted. A woman in a purple robe centered her nose in the gap, a cigarette dangling from her lower lip.

"Good morning, ma'am. I'm Officer Charles." He tapped the decorative badge on his shirt pocket. "I'm investigating a crime at the mall. This was left at the scene." He held out the pink coat.

The woman took a long drag on the cigarette and blew smoke through the door gap. "So?"

"We have reason to believe that the coat belongs to your daughter."

"*My* daughter? I don't think so."

"We think so. She's the primary suspect."

"The primary suspect? Shut up! You've got the wrong house."

"Afraid not, ma'am. The address is in the coat. We can resolve this peacefully, or I'll have to call the police."

"The police? I thought you were the police."

"Not exactly, ma'am. I work for mall security."

She took another drag, this time blowing smoke through her nose. "Then I'll be sure not to shop at the mall. I have to go."

"Not yet, ma'am. Not until I get some answers. First off, the last name on your mailbox is different than your daughter's. Have you remarried?"

"Look, I don't have time for this. Get off my porch."

"No, you look. I asked a question. I'm not leaving until I get an answer."

The woman glared, then softened her expression. "Fine. You got me. I'm divorced. I took back my maiden name."

She closed the inner door to unlatch the safety chain, then opened it wide, the storm door still between them. "I do have a daughter," she continued, "and a dog. Now, you've got until three to get lost."

Mr. Charles smirked, confident in his investigative skills. He folded his arms around the pink coat. "Allow me, ma'am. One. Two. Three."

The woman raised her brows and smiled. "Have it your way," she said opening the storm door wide. "Sic 'im, Paco!"

Mr. Charles heard toenails against hardwood. A Doberman appeared in the lurch and lunged through the doorway. Mr. Charles dropped the coat and dashed for the gate, getting bit twice in the buttocks before diving over the fence.

He landed on his shoulder and rolled in the snow cursing. The barking Doberman perched its forepaws on the fence above the BEWARE OF DOG sign.

"Good boy, Paco. Inside!" The dog obediently responded, pausing briefly on the porch to sniff Harley's coat.

Mr. Charles limped to his car and drove away, less confident in his investigative skills.

〰∞〰

Jerome sat on the crinkly rollout paper covering the exam table, again stripped to his boxers. His Santa pants and checkered shirt rested in a heap on the floor. The grungy blanket was gone, thrown into the dumpster by a nurse.

He was exhausted. He had answered all the rookie's questions and been probed by doctors. He was ready to go home for nappy time.

The Percocet was starting to take its pleasant effect. Jerome's head no longer buzzed. It chimed. He was thirsty, but not for warm water from the sink faucet.

He scooted off the table. The paper stuck to his bare thighs, reminding him of his unclothed status. It would be silly to leave the room wearing just underwear, so he tore the paper into a towel-sized sheet and wrapped it around his waist.

Jerome staggered into the hallway, finding a drinking fountain near a group of happy laughing people who got happier each time he waved. He was happy, too, until the nurse escorted him back to the room. She brought him ice chips in a cup.

Jerome stood at the window chewing ice. His mind was getting fuzzier. He saw a happy crippled man get on a bus, a curious light hovering over him. Jerome wanted to follow, but he had to get dressed first. He kneeled by his clothes, laying the ice cup on its side. The ice formed tiny clear sculptures on the carpet. Jerome gazed at the melting drips, and thought about icebergs.

He wiped the carpet with his shirt. The checkers were a blur.

Why don't Eskimos wear diamonds? he wondered as the shirt got heavy. He smelled it. It smelled of Luis. He lay down and began to chant, his already faint voice fading with each repeated phrase. "Pepé LePew. We smell you. Pepé LePew. We smell you."

The nurse found Jerome asleep on a wet carpet, and covered him with a smock. She dabbed the puddle on the floor with a white tissue to make sure the liquid was clear, not amber.

⁓⊙⊙⁓

The beautiful woman entered the supermarket but did not get a shopping cart. She smiled as she passed Bill, heading toward the back.

"Mind if I take a break?" Bill asked the checker.

"No. Go ahead."

Bill used a cart as a walker to go to the entrance, nonchalantly looking for the woman as he wheeled along. He went through the automatic door, and waited on the sidewalk a few paces outside. The air was crisp as a refrigerated apple. He scanned the cars in the lot, trying to guess which was hers.

Within a few minutes the automatic door hissed opened. The woman exited the store, pharmacy bag in hand. Bill looked away, directing his gaze to the shopping-cart handle, watching his finger draw loops across the cold plastic grip.

"Hello again," she said, putting him at ease. "Nice day, huh?"

"If you like the cold."

"I don't mind it. I like the change of seasons."

"I'm still not used to it," he answered.

"I guess that means you're not from around here?"

"My wife was." Bill had talked himself into an undesired corner.

"I'm Roberta," she said, holding out her hand. "Robbie for short."

"Bill," he said taking her hand but quickly letting go. "Watch your step on the ice."

"I will if you will." Robbie stepped off the walk onto tire-packed snow and trudged across the lot to a car with the engine running. A haggard man dozed in the back seat of her car, his face pressed against the window. Drool from his open mouth trickled down the glass.

Bill now understood what made the woman so kind and empathetic. Apparently she had a great burden of her own, caring for someone worse off than he.

⚜

Jerome's wife answered the phone on the first ring so that her medicated husband would stay asleep. It had taken all afternoon to wrestle him into bed.

"Hello."

"Is Jerome there?"

"He's not available. Can I tell him who called?"

"It's his bag boy. I got some news for him."

"He can't talk right now. He's asleep."

"Then you tell him—" Loud gleeful shrills drowned his voice.

"Tell him what?"

"Tell him that the package has been delivered," he yelled above the noise.

"What package? What are you talking about?"

"He'll know. And tell him the girls can't wait to thank him personally."

The phone clicked. She didn't know if she should be shocked or angered by the call. He never told her anything, so it was easy to imagine the worst possible. Drugs? Solicitation? Mafiosos?

As soon as he got better she would kill him.

⚜

The owner of the corner store cradled the receiver as he watched two giddy little girls dance around his store in their brand new coats from Santa.

Day Twenty-Two, Wednesday

Bill rested against the wall, temporarily surrendering his crutches to the PT's assistant. After more than a year he was graduating to a tripod cane given in recognition of his diligent efforts and kind heart. The used cane was nothing fancy, but Bill considered it a work of art.

He wiggled his fingers over the handle like a spaghetti-western cowboy preparing to unholster his gun. When he felt ready, he grasped the handle, bumped away from the wall and shifted his weight onto the cane. He proceeded deliberately, setting each foot firmly before lifting the other.

With exhausting effort he made it to the opposite wall and tried to turn.

"That's enough for today," advised the assistant. "It'll take weeks to wean you from the crutches. There's no rush."

"Next year, I'll carry you piggy back," he responded.

※◎※

Jerome rested in bed, dulled by medication and daytime TV. He had had his fill of soaps, talk shows and personal-injury attorney ads. The cooking segment on the noon news was even worse. He had no interest in wok-fried lentils and sprouts.

He thought about his students and inwardly admitted he missed them. He also thought about his Santa stint. That he did not miss, but he wasn't ready to give up the extra cash.

This would be the second workday he had missed. His tenure at school, although dead-ended, was secure, but if he didn't return to the mall soon, Moreen would hire someone else to fill his prime Pole position.

A little makeup would hide the bumps and scrapes. The only monkey wrench was getting another monkey suit. Fat chance other Santas would lend him theirs. He wouldn't, why would they?

Jerome had to find a new suit. He rolled to the edge of the bed, pulled the phonebook from the nightstand, and searched under COSTUMES, and THEATRICAL EQUIPMENT & SUPPLIES, and WIGS, and UNIFORMS. He made a number of calls, but no one in town had a Santa suit for rent or sale. He did find a vendor who had a toll-free number for Chuckles' Clown Emporium.

After ten or more rings, a woman answered with a simple hello.

"Is this Chuckles?"

"Do I sound like Chuckles? Hold on."

"No, I meant is this—" Jerome stopped the explanation when he realized she had put down the phone. Over the line he heard a door open.

"Gene! Telephone!" yelled her distant voice.

After a few minutes, Jerome heard the door again, then boots on the floor. Gene a.k.a. Chuckles picked up the phone, and soon was promoting the availability and quality of his Santa suits. After a slick presentation and the promise of overnight delivery, Jerome gave his credit card number and address. A new suit would be delivered tomorrow, money-back guaranteed.

Jerome set the phone on the receiver and returned his attention to the noon news.

"Have you seen this man?" asked the anchor with his raspy TV voice.

A series of grainy black-and-white videographs choppily flashed onto the screen, showing Santa in a C-store brandishing a pistol above his head.

"Santa Claus has traded bell ringing for gun slinging. The jolly old elf has been involved in a rash of robberies, from mini-markets to liquor stores. However, authorities believe that this thief might not be the real Santa, since he uses the door instead of the chimney, and takes more than cookies and milk. Now, if you happen to see Santa, here's how you can tell if he's the real McCoy: Look for pants. This thief was only able to steal the top half of a Santa suit. He lacks the matching red trousers."

The anchor finished with a franchised smile and nod before Jerome shut off the television.

∽○∾

Harley pressed her face against the cold glass door to peer inside the mall. She couldn't see Moron anywhere, but she still feared an ambush. If she could retrieve her lost coat another girl could use it.

"Okay. Let's go," Harley said to Boo. They squeezed through the door and sneaked along a wall, keeping a sharp lookout. Harley felt obliged to thank Santa for the new coats, even at the risk of Moron whisking her off to jail.

The bright colors of their new coats made the girls easy to spot. Harley's was tulip purple. Boo's, daffodil yellow. They approached the

North Pole but stayed far from the fountain, waiting behind a large planter with a palm-leaf bush until no one was in line. When the coast was clear, Harley let Boo run to Santa. She climbed into his lap, digging her bony little knees into his thighs.

"Ouch," he said. "What's your name, sweetheart?"

The voice didn't sound right to Boo. She stared at his eyes. They didn't look right either. She puckered her face into a pug-nosed scowl.

She knew Santa Claus. Santa was a friend of hers. This pretender was no Santa Claus.

Boo squirmed to get off the stranger's lap, but he grabbed her arms to pull her back. They grappled for a moment, then she started to scream.

"Lego! Lego moms!"

"Now, now, it's okay. Don't you want to talk to Santa?"

"Lego! Ewe lego!" Boo arched her back to worm out of the stranger's grip. Her coat and shirt bunched above her bare tummy.

The camera flashed.

"Sorry," apologized the elf. "My mistake."

Boo continued to kick and wiggle until the stranger set her free. She scrambled to a safe distance, then reeled to face the impostor. Her shirt and coat were bunched to her armpits. Her belly stuck out like a knotted balloon.

"Ewe knot Sand Claws!" she yelled, pointing a finger at him. "Ewe baa men!"

Santa straightened his coat sleeves and beard. He looked down his nose at Harley. "Did you want to talk to me?"

"No. We just came to say thanks for the coats. Thanks for the coats."

Boo continued to scowl at the stranger even after the girls left the porch. They stopped halfway to the exit.

"We can't go home yet. We need to say good-bye to the janitor."

"Hymn gift summon knee foe Chrysalis?"

"No. No more money. Moron is after us."

"Duh mink wean?"

"Right. The Mean Queen. We have to watch out for her and King Wiener."

The girls turned back, hugging the wall until they saw Mr. Ludwig in the food court. He scattered sawdust from a box like chicken feed. They headed for him through a maze of tables, dodging people with trays of marvelously odorous food. The blend of smells was torture— french fries, hot dogs, gyros, cinnamon rolls—with a hint of pine in the air. Harley salivated like Pavlov's dog until she smelled the sour stench near Mr. Ludwig.

Boo pinched her nose. "Poop," she observed.

"Nope. Barf," Mr. Ludwig clarified. "Let's go over there, away from the smell." He led the girls to a bench at the edge of the food court. "Love your coats," he complimented. "Very, very nice."

"Santa gave them to us. We came and told him thanks."

Boo agreed. "Sam Clocks cave dam toss."

"Santa gave you coats? Our Santa?"

"I think so. He left them at a store by our house, and his friend gave them to us."

"At least that's what this friend told you, right? Maybe it's the friend that needs a thanking."

Harley thought for a moment. "No. His friend doesn't sell coats. I think they came from Santa."

"Maybe. Maybe not. But I sure like those colors."

Harley rubbed her sleeve. "Purple's okay, I guess. I like green better."

"Green? I think purple looks good on you."

"Green is God's favorite color."

"Says who?"

"My mom."

"Why would green be God's favorite? What about blue? Or red?"

"Dad says God likes blue, but I think He likes green the best. When it's warm outside, everything is green. God likes green."

"Then why does your dad say God likes blue?"

"Because he says you only see green when you look down, but things are blue when you look up."

Boo interjected. "Eye light blew."

"Me, too," said Mr. Ludwig. "And green, and black, and white, and brown. Look."

He draped Boo's small fingers over his bare wrist, then he put Harley's hand next to Boo's. The comparative flesh tones were distinct.

"See? You're not green and Boo's not blue, and I'm not purple—

except when I get really cold. God made us different colors, so He must like them all the same."

Boo drummed her fingers on the janitor's wrist, but Harley slipped her hand away.

"We have to go," she said.

"Can I buy you a hamburger first?"

"Yeah," hooted Boo, sliding off the bench to jump up and down.

"We can't," answered Harley, trying to ignore the engulfing scents around her.

"Too late. Boo said yes. You can eat them at home." He took Boo's hand and walked into the food court.

Harley shook her head, but her feet followed. "Boo likes ketchup only, please," she said.

"How about you?"

"I like ketchup, pickles and lettuce."

"Green stuff," Mr. Ludwig observed.

Green stuff, thought Harley. She *did* like green stuff, just like mom. She added to her order.

"I'll try a tomato. Red is a good color, too."

⟲⊙⟳

The apartment had been dark for hours, but it still wasn't officially bedtime. The girls sat on their mattress sucking candy canes. Harley licked hers to a sharp point, but wouldn't let Boo do the same because it would poke her eye out.

When there was nothing left to do, the girls got under the covers. Harley wanted to escape into a dream but she wasn't tired enough. She lay on her stomach, stroking her finger on the empty money carton by the mattress. Her plan to replace the money spent on the poor woman was now impossible. She flicked wax flakes off the carton while she filtered street sounds to listen for her father. Boo fought sleep, hugging Baby Bear.

"Eye needle same eye players," she whined.

"Okay. Kneel down. Do you need help?"

"No." Boo rotated onto her knees, keeping her backside blanketed. She folded her arms around Baby Bear. "Farther Haven. Fangs phone ice day. Fangs foe newt goats. Ant fangs forum boogers. Police bliss Tatty, ant Hurry, ant Bevy Bayer."

She paused to think. Harley interrupted. "Please bless Marci."

Boo opened one eye. "Shhh!" she scolded. "Eye finking."

"Sorry."

Boo closed her eye and continued. "Police bliss Mossy. Ant police bliss Sam Clods target a tofu Hurry's buff day. Almond."

"Good job. Now go to sleep."

Boo pulled the blankets to her neck and closed her eyes for good. Harley continued to pick at the empty carton, thinking about how foolish she had been to follow the star. She looked over, amazed at how quickly Boo could fall asleep, then she slipped from the blankets and went to the window to find the star. Its light burned her eyes, making them water. Prism tears stretched strands of light from her nose to the star, but try as she might she couldn't touch the elusive beams.

Jerome made three phone calls before breakfast. The first was to the school to request sick leave for the rest of the week. Even though he felt better, he wasn't in peak shape for teaching. Next, he called Chuckles to confirm shipment of his Santa suit. The third call was to Moreen at home. Her phone rang six times.

"Hello," she answered groggily.

"Moreen?"

"Yes."

"This is Jerome. I hope I didn't wake you from your beauty sleep," he said. *Because, oh how you need it,* he thought.

"Why would I be asleep at this early hour?" she asked sarcastically. "I'm always up before dawn to watch the farm report. Now, speak your business so I can get back to milking cows."

"You have cows?" he teased, knowing Moron would nibble at the dangling line.

"No, I do not have cows, you idiot! How could I have cows? I live within city limits."

"But you said—"

"I know what I said! I only said it because you were stupid enough to ask if you woke me up. Of course you woke me up!"

"Oh, I'm sorry. I'll call back when you're awake."

"No, Jerome. Do not call back. Tell me what you want, right now."

"I just wanted to tell you I will be in this afternoon with my brand-spanking-new Santa suit. You won't need to hire a scab."

"Fine, Jerome. I won't hire a scab. Anything else?"

"Well, yes, there is one thing. Moreen . . ."

"What, Jerome?" she demanded.

"What are you wearing?" he cooed.

The phone call bungled to a hush. Jerome made her smile. He knew it.

"Good-bye, Jerome," she finally answered. "See you this afternoon."

By two o'clock Jerome had called Chuckles five times. Each time he was told that the suit had been shipped via overnight express and that it should have been delivered already. There was nothing else that Jerome could do except let Moreen know that a scab was needed after all. He dialed the mall over and over, getting a busy signal each time. Moreen's home phone only had voice messaging. He no longer had her cell or pager numbers thanks to the suit snatchers.

Jerome tried the mall again. The line was still busy.

"Great!" he said.

He'd have to deliver his message of unavailability in person. While he was out and about he might as well replace Annie's blanket. He went to the linen closet and pulled four blankets, but none was as warm as the comforter on his bed. He bunched it into a wad, then loaded all five blankets into the trunk of his car. Before leaving he called the mall one last time. Still busy.

Jerome backed out of the garage and headed for the mall. Billowy clouds rolled across the graying sky, threatening a storm. Bare trees reached for the obscured sun, their limbs raised in supplication for Spring. Wind gusts tugged at the steering wheel and whistled through the wiper blades. Jerome thought about delivering the blankets first, but knew Moreen would be angry enough already. He stayed on course for the mall, passing the chapel and its lawn crèche with Baby Jesus in a birdbath.

Jerome pressed hard on the brakes, skidding to a hard stop. He backed along the curb until he was directly in front of the church. Sure enough, the infant Christ had been put in a birdbath manger.

He didn't laugh or even smile.

That's not right, he thought. *That really is not right.*

He got out and hurried across the snowy lawn, unable to believe that everyone else had failed to notice the misplaced Christ. Had the Child been like this all night, or had He been defiled in broad daylight? Either way, the act aggravated him. Even the prior pranks were no longer amusing.

Jerome reached for the ceramic Christ but stopped to admire the detailed paint work. Someone with steady hand and heart had taken great care to paint the Child with natural living colors. Each part of the tiny body was perfect. The brush strokes were nearly invisible. The fingernails and dimples on the delicate hands were a tone lighter than the surrounding skin. Curls on the Child's head had been painted without any overlap onto the cherubic face. The swaddling cloth was an eggshell white, with minuscule Hebraic letters dot-painted to look like stitchery.

The multi-brown hazel eyes were inspiring as they gazed toward heaven. Jerome thought it a pity that passersby couldn't see this devout detail from afar. He carefully returned the Child to the manger, then hefted the heavy plaster birdbath to the trash bin around the side, hobbling and huffing as he went. He still felt the effects of his beating.

He heard children playing in a fenced playground to the back.

"Go look for Boo," he thought.

He took a step toward the playground, but stopped because he was running late. He turned to leave, rocking between his car and the playground. Finally, he compromised by going to the door. Knocking as he entered, he called out.

"Anybody home?"

"Nope. We're all here at preschool," said the red-haired teacher. "What can I do for you?"

"I'm looking for a little girl named Boo. What's the chance of her being enrolled here?"

"Did you say a little ghoul?" she answered. "Sorry. That was bad, but I couldn't resist. You know, our records are private, and I couldn't disclose information about our students without authorization. But off the record, there's no one here named Boo."

"How about Harley?"

"Harley?" She shook her head. "It must be some other daycare."

"No harm in asking. Mind if I use your phone for a quick local call?" He still hoped to avoid facing Moreen.

"I don't think they're working." She picked up the wall phone and put it to her ear. "Nope. Still down."

"C'est la guerre. Thanks anyway." He stepped to the door, inspecting the coats along the wall as he went. There was no yellow coat like the one he bought for Boo. He stepped into the cold and walked along the sidewalk to the street, paying no attention to the fading playground voices behind him.

"Marci!" a teacher yelled. "If you can't sit down, you'll have to get off the slide!"

"Sully," she apologized, her familiar voice just one step beyond Jerome's auditory range.

※

Jerome hurried into the mall, walking fast but not jogging. He wiped his shoes on the soaked floor mat before stepping across the slick tiles. From the entrance he could see the empty Santa throne. No children were in line. The elf sat on the counter, dangling his feet and banging his bell-toed slippers against the panel.

"Holy mistletoe, Batman!" said the elf, slamming a fist into his palm. "Where's your mask and cape?"

"My package didn't arrive. I won't be playing Batman today. Where's Cat Woman?"

"In the litter box. She'll be right back to claw your eyes out."

"I tried to call, but the bat phones have been on the fritz."

"Yup. The Penguin and Cat Woman have been throwing conniptions all afternoon. She won't be happy when she sees Bruce Wayne."

"I take it the other Santa has gone?"

"Yup."

"And Moron doesn't have a backup for me?"

"Nope." The elf reached into his pocket. "Here, I got you a present. You'll like this." He handed Jerome a photo of Boo wrestling with another Santa. Jerome grinned as he sat on the counter next to the elf.

"What a peach! You took this for me?"

"Of course. Merry Christmas. On one condition."

"What?"

"Do your royal proclamation."

Jerome cleared his throat and extended his arm to oblige. "Announcing his Royal Majesty, Prince Snotty, Earl of Our Lady of Goatedumb!"

"Ahem," responded a female voice from behind.

They both looked over their shoulders. Moreen stood on the other side of the counter, her arms folded tightly.

"Hello, Moreen," Jerome saluted. "It's about time you got here."

"You're late. Get dressed."

"I can't. I've been trying to call you all afternoon. There's been a slight delay in the delivery of my suit."

Moreen clenched her jaw. Her eyebrows curled down. The tint of her cheeks deepened. She scraped her teeth over her lower lip, then looked him in the eyes.

"You told me this morning that you had, and I quote, a brand-spanking-new suit, end quote, so I wouldn't have to hire a quote, scab, end quote." She paused to scratch the corner of her mouth, then went on. "And now you tell me that you don't have a brand-spanking-new suit."

"I would say that's pretty accurate."

Jerome was now a puppy by a puddle, about to get whacked with a newspaper. The elf saw what was coming and snuck off to sweep cobwebs from the throne.

Moreen stood quiet for a moment, relaxing the muscles in her face. She became calm enough to give Jerome a glint of hope.

"I'm really sorry, Moreen. I tried to call, but I didn't have your cell number. What can I do to make it right?"

"Don't worry about it, Jerome. Apology accepted," she said. "Truth is, I was just about to fire you, but we've been together a long time. It would take a lot more than this to get you fired."

"Thank you, Moreen. I really, truly appreciate this."

"Yes sir, it would take *a lot* more," she continued, barely taking a breath. "It would take something like shoving me into the fountain to protect a little thief. Or being rude to Scotty. Or infesting the mall with mosquitoes. That's what it would take to justify firing you."

Jerome studied her face. His Santa stint was over. He decided to leave in a blaze of glory.

"You forgot to mention getting your car towed, and calling you and your pig-faced brother names behind your back."

Moreen's eyes bulged. Jerome leaned toward her.

"Me Tarzan. You Moron. Go ahead, fire me. But remember, I know all your dirty little secrets. So if there's nothing else, I'll be over in the fountain, waiting for my final paycheck—without any unauthorized deductions."

"What dirty little secrets? What are you inferring?"

"Don't be cute, Moreen. You know exactly what I'm talking about. You forget I was here back then."

Jerome turned and walked away but Moreen didn't move. She tried to recollect skeletons in her closet that he could resurrect. She couldn't be sure he was bluffing. She retreated to the office to prepare a check.

In truth, Jerome knew nothing, but he couldn't help jabbing her one last time. He went to the fountain and listened to the percolating water while he enjoyed Boo's candid moment. He put the photo in his shirt pocket, and removed his shoes and socks. The floor tiles were cool and refreshing against his naked toes. He straddled the rim and stepped into the fountain. The temperature was well below spa standards. A shiver raced up his spine, making his shoulders quiver. He looked to see if anyone was watching, embarrassed by the reflex.

With sock in hand, he dipped his arm past his elbow to gather coins. His pants soaked to mid-thigh, and his sleeves to his biceps. When the first sock was filled, he looped a knot in it and grabbed the other. When the second sock was filled, he started putting coins in his pants.

Both Mr. Ludwig and Mr. Charles responded to the call about the loon in the fountain. When the janitor saw who it was, he convinced security to back off unless Jerome got belligerent.

"Are you sober?" Mr. Ludwig asked.

"Do I look sober?"

"No."

"I'm as dry as a summer sidewalk, except my pants. Look. I wet myself." Jerome started to sing.

"*How dry I am,*
How wet I'll be . . ."

Mr. Ludwig rolled his eyes. "Can I assume you're gathering coins for our favorite charity?"

"You know it. Come on in. I could use another sock."

The janitor looked at his shoes, then pressed his toe against each heel and stepped out of them. He tugged off both socks. "I'm not coming in, but you can have the socks."

"Thank you kindly. Could you talk Moreen out of her panty hose?"

⋘◯◯⋙

Jerome sat in the passenger seat with the heater on full blast, the vent louvers aimed at his soaked pants. Every so often he turned his bottom to the vent to dry his underside. His shoes were wedged in the steering wheel to dry the damp lining. His last paycheck rested on the dash. Four wet socks filled with coins were on the back seat. The car reeked of humid chlorine.

Wind rocked the car on its tires as thick clouds churned on an upper air stream. Another storm was due before dusk. He scooted to the driver's seat, tossing his shoes aside. His toes felt at home curled over the pedals.

He drove under the traffic signal where he had seen the green gumdrops turn to yellow. A fleeting thought passed through his mind about the flickering light and the raggedy dark-winged angel, Annie. As he passed the spot where the fall occurred, renewed guilt arose for not having stopped to help the man with crutches. He turned left at the pet store and circled the block, parking by an abandoned building with a sagging chain-link fence around a yard cluttered with snow-laden rubbish. The urban cave was dark, unrevealing of the lives it sheltered.

Jerome slipped his bare feet into his shoes, and put on his coat before shutting off the engine. He gripped the key before opening the door, and released the trunk latch as he stepped out. Locking the car with the keys, he placed them in his pant pocket.

His eyes alert for potential assailants, he got the blankets from the trunk and slammed it shut, then hurried to a corner of the fence covered with shrubbery. Pulling on the loose mesh, he squeezed through and followed a trail between rubbish piles that led to the building. There he opened a creased plywood sheet hinged with nails on one side that blocked the entrance.

"Annie?" he called, poking his head under the plywood.

No answer. He slipped inside.

"Ike? Rat? Anybody home?"

No answer.

The plywood slapped closed, blocking the dusk from the dark foyer. Jerome blinked a few times, opening his eyes wide to adjust to the dim light. He listened for life that he couldn't see.

"It's me, Jerome. I brought some blankets."

No answer. The floor creaked. He reeled to face the noise, clutching the blankets to his chest. The sound of breathing heightened his fear, until he realized it was his own.

"Luis?" Jerome whimpered.

The plywood door cracked. Jerome lurched deeper into the dark foyer, but stopped when Ike pushed through the entrance.

"Ike! You scared me to death!"

"Who are you?"

"Jerome. The Santa guy. I brought you blankets."

"That's pretty asinine, don't you think? Apparently you didn't learn anything from your last outing."

"I learned that it's cold. I didn't want to leave Annie without a blanket."

"Annie's tougher than you think. She takes care of herself. And what she can't do, we do."

"Is she around?"

"No. She left to go see her boys."

"Home for Christmas? That's great."

"It's not what you think. She goes to see them. She watches from the street, through the window, and leaves them something on their porch for Christmas. Then she comes back and tells us all about her boys and her grandkids. But she doesn't ever bother them."

"*Bother* them! How could she bother her boys? Are they too good to have their mom for Christmas?"

"No, she just won't have it."

"Why won't she?"

"Why *should* she?"

"I don't know. I mean, she'd be so close to them, just on the other side of the window. Why wouldn't she knock and go in? She wouldn't have to stay."

"You don't know Annie. She doesn't want to be seen. She wants her boys to remember her as she was, not as she is. Women get that way, worrying about how they look, like who's going to style their hair and do their makeup when they're laid to rest in a pine box. They get to a point where they don't like what they see in the mirror, and some, like Annie, want to see things only from one side of the glass—kind of like Alice in Wonderland, but they feel like they can never go back."

"What about you? Do you feel like you can never go back?"

"I don't have a boy to go back to. At least Annie's got a window."

Jerome felt the chill on his ankles. "I had no idea," he apologized. "Where should we put the blankets?"

"Let's put them on a pallet to keep them off the floor."

Ike took the blankets and went into the hallway. Jerome followed him to the familiar room with boarded windows and the fire barrel.

"You want me to help start a fire?" Jerome offered.

"Too early. We wait until people are in bed. That way we keep a low profile. Fewer calls to the cops."

Jerome thought Ike a curious creature. He was articulate and attractive. Not that Jerome was interested, but from a man's perspective of what a woman's perspective might be, Ike had handsome features under the grime.

"Do you have any family, Ike? Parents or anything?"

"Just a sister and an ex-wife."

"Ever contact your sister?"

"Who'd want to? Her husband's a dink. I don't even know where they live, they move all the time. He couldn't stay in one place to save his life. For that matter, neither can I. I'm nomadic."

"Pardon?"

"*Nomadic*. I'm a nomad. A wanderer and a vagabond. A hobo." Ike smiled. "Did you ever see Red Skelton do his hobo routine? Wasn't that a hoot?"

Jerome nodded. "My dad loved Red Skelton, rest his soul."

"Whose? Your dad's or Red Skelton's?"

"Both. But Red Skelton was funnier."

"Remember when it was safe to go trick-or-treating?" Ike asked, boarding a runaway train of thought. "Whenever I couldn't think of anything to be for Halloween, I always went as a hobo. I must have been a hobo every other year. Remember that plastic hobo mask, with a stogie in the mouth, and the elastic band that would pinch your ears? And the mouth had a slit in it so you could stick your tongue through?"

Jerome remembered. He, too, had been a hobo many times. It was everyone's last-resort costume.

"Maybe I should have dressed up like a lawyer," Ike continued. "Then I wouldn't be a hobo. But lawyers weren't scary when we were kids, like they are now. Or pious." Ike held two fingers over his heart and looked to heaven, taking an icon pose. "Trick-or-treat, kiss my feet."

"You got burned by your ex-, didn't you?" Jerome asked. "Her attorney took you to the cleaners."

"No. I *gave* her the cleaners. But her attorney *was* a jerk. They don't teach that in law school. It's inbred."

"Why did you give in?"

"I loved her. *She* fell out of love, not me. In her mind, I was the cause of what happened to Elijah. She blamed everyone, starting with the doctors and ending with me."

Jerome kicked the fire barrel, pretending to look for embers, but really staring at the empty chair. He wanted to change the topic.

"How long were you in the service?"

"Never."

"Then what's with the fatigues? I thought you were some combat-happy soldier with extreme stress syndrome."

"The only combat I saw was with my wife. These fatigues are a costume. I once got beat up, like you, so I started wearing fatigues and acting edgy. No one bothers me anymore. If your Santa suit had been khaki, you wouldn't have been mugged."

"You think?"

"Maybe not. You'd look like a wuss no matter what you wore."

"Have you ever tried to go back? You're missing a lot of life out here."

"Am I? Life is better here than behind some desk. I don't destroy anyone's life out here."

"That doesn't mean you contribute."

"Sure I do. You don't think Annie or Luis—or even you—need me? Think about it. What would happen to the likes of you if we hobos were pushing papers around some leather-top desk while you were getting your dance card punched over in the park? Here's where I do the most good."

The chill on Jerome's ankles was gone, warmed by the conversation.

"I better get going. It's dark and I'm not in khaki. Will you make sure Annie gets the best blanket?"

"Sure."

As they stepped outside, Jerome noticed the horizon. Patchy clouds had separated in the east, letting a host of stars push through the darkness.

"So when do you think Annie will get back?"

"Any day, but I can't say exactly."

"Is there anything else she needs? Is there anything you need?"

"Not really. Just say hello if you pass me on the street. Nothing is worse than being ignored. Tell me *no* when I pander, but don't look through me like I'm invisible."

"You need gloves or anything? You're talking to Santa, you know."

"You're not Santa. Santa's not stupid enough to come to this neighborhood. He only goes to houses with money."

"So I'll make an unscheduled stop."

"Stop whenever you want. Mi casa es su casa."

Jerome thought about the invitation. Ike really meant it.

"Okay. How about Sunday? Will Annie be back by Sunday?"

"Should be."

"Then I'll see you Sunday morning," Jerome answered with a plan. "Look for me on this side of the park at eight in the morning straight up."

Ike bent his left arm to look at his dirty wrist. He tapped his bare wrist, then held it to his ear. "My watch seems to have stopped. You'll forgive me if I'm late."

Day Twenty-Four, Friday

Jerome sat at the kitchen table with paper and pen, trying to summarize all he knew about the girls. He stared at the photo of Boo. In his mind he listened to her small voice.

"Tatty bloke hiss lakes. Tatty half ass dent."

He wrote:

> FATHER
> bum legs

Jerome visualized the man with crutches struggling to cross the street. He remembered the beads of sweat and the doubled sweatshirts. Jerome added *needs coat?* and *church guy?* to the list, believing he had to be the girls' father. Why had he lied about knowing Harley? Maybe she told him about being stalked by Santa, or maybe the man really didn't know her. Jerome listed things he knew about Harley:

> HARLEY
> lives by store
> bad neighborhood
> saw near church
> no xmas last year
> coat
> lady & kids, old bldg
> money in milk carton

Jerome remembered the time he saw Harley walking by herself, but both girls appeared at the mall together. He put *w/o Boo* after *saw near church*. Soon the paper was filled with tidbits of apparently unrelated information. The common threads were few. The church, the mall, and the neighborhood all held answers, but nothing jumped off the page. He closed his eyes to hear Boo again.

"Iguana tofu Hurry's buffed egg."

He replayed the request until the meaning came clear. Boo wanted a toy for Harley's birthday to replace Baby Bear. He wrote *wants toy for H's b-day* and *—stuffed bear?* under Boo's name. Below Harley's name he added *wants present for Boo*.

The lists now read:

FATHER	HARLEY
bum legs	lives by store
needs coat?	bad neighborhood
church guy?	saw near church w/o Boo
went to neighborhood	no xmas last year
Annie helped?	coat
bus rider	lady & kids, old bldg
—by mall	money in milk carton
—by clinic?	school book
	mall rat on school days
	wants present for Boo

BOO	MOM
babysitter near mall	dead?
church daycare	
—no coat	
Baby Bear	
wants toy for H's b-day	
—stuffed bear?	

Jerome had to find where the girls lived. This was, after all, what Christmas was all about. He got in his car to piece together all the clues he could. Soon he had circled blocks near the church in search of Harley's school. Finding nothing, he searched Harley's neighborhood.

Maybe Harley rode the bus to school. Jerome returned to the church and found the nearest bus stop. He scribbled down route numbers from the sign, then proceeded to the mall and walked along the sidewalk to note the routes there. The exhaust from idling buses nauseated him, but he finished his list and checked it twice: 2, 3, 5, 9, 11, 17, 18, 24, 32, 38, 40, and 41. He drew boxes around 17, 18, and 41, putting a steeple on each.

An orange-haired man paced nearby. The man's spastic arm and gnarly fist were pressed to his ribs like a duck wing. In his good arm he held an infant girl close to his chest. He wore a warm leather coat, but the baby was wrapped only in a receiving blanket. Repeatedly, he tucked the infant's dangling arm under his neck, but never made any effort to cover her with the blanket.

That's shameful, Jerome thought. *She should have a coat.*

Jerome became angry when he noticed that the man also wore a gold bracelet. He prepared to flail him verbally for treating his daughter like a doll, and stepped forward for a confrontation. As he inhaled to speak, he noticed that the infant didn't move on her own. The man wasn't treating a baby like a doll, he was treating a doll like a baby.

He walked past the man without saying anything. *No more judgments today,* he thought. *Maybe tomorrow.*

He drove to the hospital to write down the bus routes near the clinic where he, in a drug-induced delusion, had seen a halo over a bus. With all the routes recorded on paper, he narrowed the list to one bus.

⬥

Seated on stacked bags of dog food, Bill tied two plastic bags of groceries to each handle of his crutches. He borrowed masking tape from the assistant manager to strap the bags to the crutch poles to keep them from banging against his legs. Never had he tried to take home so many groceries from so great a distance, but the supermarket prices were significantly better than those of the corner store near his apartment.

With his first step Bill worried about the weight on the loaded crutches, but he put his faith in his feeble feet. Each forward lift of the crutches exerted more pressure on his ankles. By the time he got halfway across the parking lot, Bill knew he didn't have enough strength. He could make it to the bus stop by the supermarket, but he would never make it from the mall to home.

He might be able to stash the goods at the church, but even that would spend his strength.

"Can I help you to your car?"

Bill looked to his right. Robbie was standing beside him. She touched his elbow.

"I don't have a car right now. I'm just heading to the bus stop there." He pointed the direction with his nose. "I should be okay."

"You sure? I'd be happy to help."

"I'll be fine, thanks."

"Okay," she answered. "Have a nice evening."

Robbie dropped her hand from his elbow but stayed at his side, watching him, calling his bluff, waiting for him to show his mettle. Bill didn't dare move for fear she would see his physical weakness, but he feared more that she might notice his weakness for her.

"When you get off the bus, how far do you have to go?" Robbie asked.

"Not far. Maybe half a block."

"*Maybe* half a block? Does that mean maybe a whole block, or maybe half a mile? How far exactly?"

"I'll be fine. I have daughters that can help."

"How old?"

Bill didn't want to answer. "I'll be fine, really."

Robbie reached down and began to strip tape off the bags. "Come on. I'll give you a ride home."

"I can't, really."

"Sure you can. If you could make it to that bus stop, you can make it to my car. Especially since I'm carrying your groceries." Robbie continued to pull tape off the bags and crutches, and within seconds had the four bags in her grasp.

"I don't want to impose," Bill said.

"Then let's go. It would be easier now to drive you home than to re-tape these bags to your crutches."

Bill felt his throat tighten. He coughed to open his airway, and took a deep breath before following Robbie to her car.

Jerome parked in the mall lot near the bus stops. He had called bus info and gotten the departure times for route 17, the only bus that went by both the church and the hospital. He would ride the route to see what he could see and strike up conversations. Bus drivers were just bartenders of dry pubs on wheels. They would know frequent riders and might know Harley or the man with crutches.

The route 17 bus was parked and waiting. Jerome stashed the coin socks under the seat and hurried from his car, mindful to not lock his keys inside. He stepped into the bus and dropped his pre-counted fare into the bin before surveying the unfamiliar setting. He hadn't been on a bus for years. Even as a teacher he had found ways to skip bus duty on field trips.

He waddled to the inward-facing seat directly behind the driver as the bus pulled from the curb. His fellow passengers were bland and cloaked in pale colors. They all avoided eye contact like riders on a horizontal elevator. Everyone reeked of spice. Jerome decided all bus riders were members of socially challenged groups, either old, poor, disabled, or environmentalist.

The black mat under his feet was splotched with treaded gum. A dried apple core sat wedged in a window track at his shoulder. The glass had greasy residue from a napper's hair. All the signs and ads were bilingual. The driver slowly accelerated past the line of buses parked at the curb. Jerome looked through the window at the equally drab passengers on other buses. Suddenly he caught a glimpse of purple and yellow sandwiching a gray sweatshirt in another bus. He jumped across the aisle to see if it was them. It was.

Jerome yanked the cable above the window, sounding the chime.

"What, already?" asked the driver.

"Sorry. I'm on the wrong bus."

"I can't stop here," the driver answered as he went through a green light. "There's a stop on the other side."

The bus stopped on the other side of the intersection. Jerome paused at the open door. "I need a transfer," he said.

The driver tore a ticket from the pad clipped to the visor. Jerome took it, hopped to the street, and hurried to the intersection crosswalk. He eyed the route 32 bus he wanted, watching it pull from the curb. He would have to hail it from the stop behind him. He scurried back and waited at the stop with his arm raised.

The bus turned right at the intersection. Jerome looked at the sign by his head. Route 32 wasn't among the numbers it advertised.

Over the next hour back at the mall, Jerome questioned every driver of route 32 buses about the girls and their father, until finally the right bus returned.

"Did you have two girls and a man with crutches on your last run?"

"Was the guy about this tall? With girls in yellow and purple?"

"Yeah, that's them."

"Nope. Not on my bus," said the driver with a wink.

Jerome mustered a polite laugh. "I was supposed to be with them, but I missed the bus. Can you tell me where they got off so I don't miss the party?"

"The *party*? At a cemetery?"

"It's not really a party," Jerome explained. "It's more like a wake."

"A *wake*? At a cemetery?"

Jerome shrugged, then boarded with his transfer ticket. He sat behind the driver, again feeling awkward among so many blasé people. The bus was awash in earth tones. The old man across the aisle had furrowed wrinkles in his weathered face. Gray bushes sprouted above his eyes and from his ears and nose, and thick calluses padded his chapped palms.

An old woman sat next to the old man. The wrinkles in her brow were sculpted, not plowed. She clutched a vinyl purse with one hand and the arm of the old man with the other. She caught Jerome staring at her, and looked to her husband, trying not to smile.

Jerome began to notice colors that he had initially missed. The old woman's hazel eyes were like polished brook stones. Her cheeks were smooth as ice cream, and her graying hair Chrysler-chrome blue. The old man's fingers were stained dandelion yellow from nicotine, and the cracks on his knuckles were red.

As the bus pulled away, Jerome reassessed his fellow riders. He and they were all going separate ways in the same direction. They were collectively dreary, but individually picturesque.

After a short distance the bus stopped without a chime. The door opened. No one waited at the stop.

"This is it," said the driver.

Jerome stepped off, landing a few paces from the wrought-iron gate of the city cemetery. Frost crystals blasted against his neck like grains of sand. He lowered his neck into his coat collar, and followed three sets of shoe prints and one set of crutch stabs in the snow shaded by a tall stone wall. At the entrance the snow and prints disappeared where the bright sun licked the asphalt drive. Through half-closed eyes Jerome saw acres of grave markers, with an occasional bare tree or evergreen on the landscape. A distant backhoe dug a new hole, piling dull-brown clods of frozen dirt onto a green tarp. Here and there people stood like scarecrows in breeze-blown coats, but he did not see the girls or their father.

Jerome followed the asphalt road into the heart of the cemetery. The dry asphalt showed no tell-tale prints to guide him. As he walked he analyzed sites to his left and right. At first the headstones were numerous and crooked, without recent excavations, but as he continued they became less dense. This was where he expected to find a grave less than three years old—Boo's age. A few steps farther, Jerome found a stab print inches off the right side of the path. He veered his course starboard.

Before long he found multiple prints in the snow angling across the lawn both coming and going. Jerome ran alongside, making his own trail to leave the family's prints undisturbed. At first, the girls' outbound prints paralleled those of their father, but soon his were on top of theirs, indicating they had run ahead. The prints ended at a simple granite headstone. A green-dyed carnation lay at its base.

Jerome kept his distance, envisioning the family at the grave. He sensed their lingering grief all around him like smoke from embers not fully extinguished.

He absorbed the chiseled information on the headstone.

LAURA PAIGE EDISON
Here, for us, the horizon has a setting sun.
There, for you, it has a glorious dawn.

Laura Edison was born April 23rd. She died June 6th, eighteen months ago, barely thirty years old. In the lower left corner of her headstone was an engraved vine that Jerome recognized as ivy. The winding vine formed an L shape, with tiny berries and sharp pointed leaves. The opposite corner had a thicker vine in a reverse-L shape, with broad leaves shading a single small pumpkin.

He stared at the ivy and pumpkin vines until his toes and mind were numb, then backed away, reciting the names Boo and Harley Edison until he left the cemetery. He would try the church again, even if it meant going to Sunday morning services.

❧

Jerome's wife was wrapped in an afghan curled up in the love seat in front of the TV, even cozier in her flannel pajamas and slippers. She clutched a wad of tissues, prepared to dab her eyes whenever occasion required. A mass of spent tissues was already piled on the coffee table in front of her. She cried when George kissed Mary. She cried when the Martinis moved into their new home. She cried when Mr. Potter kept the money from George.

Jerome was sure she would sob when friends with baskets of money came rolling into the Bailey home, as if she hadn't seen the movie before—this year.

He hated *It's a Wonderful Life*. He wondered what kind of bell might cause an angel to lose his wings. *A school bell*, he thought. He stood and left his wife to finish the movie alone, heading for the laundry room to iron a shirt for the morning. Jerome dug through the ironing basket when he came across Luis's freshly washed checkered shirt.

Great! He suddenly realized his scheduling dilemma.

He had promised to meet Ike at 8:00 am, but Sunday services started at 9:30. If he didn't go to church in the morning he probably would miss his chance to find the girls, unless Annie were at the park with Ike, but Ike probably wouldn't even remember, so Jerome would be wasting his time by going to the park, especially if Annie did not show.

Christmas is for children. Ike would understand. It wasn't as important to keep a loose promise to a hobo as it was to find the girls. Jerome's meeting with Ike seemed trumped by a higher cause.

Day Twenty-Six, Sunday

Ike, Rat and Luis sat on the park bench, their seats insulated with folded newspapers. Ike tugged a Mickey Mouse pocket watch from his pants, cupping it in his hand. He checked the time and snapped it closed.

"Well?" Rat asked, his warm breath gliding on the cold air.

"8:20."

"And exactly what are we doing here?"

Luis mumbled a response and stood to leave.

"You've got that right," Ike agreed. He stood to follow.

"Wait a minute. You didn't answer me. What are we doing here?"

"We were waiting for Santa Claus but he stood us up."

"Santa Claus?"

"The Santa man said to meet him here at eight. So here we are and here he isn't. Let's go."

"What did he want?"

"Doesn't matter. He isn't coming."

Ike and Luis walked to the curb. Rat waited on the bench, shoving extra newspapers under his seat. Luis stepped off the curb, and crossed the street without looking. Ike followed, but checked traffic first. It didn't take long for Rat to follow.

"Wait up," he hollered, jogging into the street.

A car turned the corner and accelerated toward him. It honked once, then honked again. Rat cursed, then he recognized the Santa man and stopped in the middle of the street. Jerome pulled up next to him.

"Sorry I'm late. I had to go back for matches."

"We got matches. You need matches?"

"Not anymore. Where's Annie and Ike?"

"Annie's not here. Ike and Luis just left. I'll get them."

Rat darted off, yelling for Ike and Luis while Jerome parked and stepped from the comfort of his warm car. The biting breeze sifted through Jerome's checkered shirt. He ducked into the car to get his coat, hat and gloves, putting them on as he danced to the trunk. He unloaded grocery bags onto the curb, and tugged out a card table. He locked the three good legs in place, and strapped the bad leg with duct tape. Annie couldn't have done better.

Rat returned with Ike and Luis.

"What's this?" Ike asked.

"Breakfast. I'm making you breakfast. Sorry I'm late. I forgot matches."

"We have matches."

"I told him already," Rat whispered.

"I went back to be safe. You guys want to give me a hand?"

Ike nodded his approval. Rat helped Jerome heft a camp stove from the trunk and sidestepped it to the table. Jerome retrieved a propane canister and hooked it to the stove. He patted all his pockets for the matches.

"Got a light?" he asked.

Ike produced a lighter and held a flame to the burners as Jerome turned knobs.

"We need water," Jerome directed, handing a speckled blue enamel kettle and a bowl to Rat. "Can you fill these, please?"

Rat hustled to the drinking fountain by the monkey bars. Jerome turned to Luis. "Would you please fill these pots?"

Luis mumbled something, but Jerome shoved the pots into his hands anyway. Luis continued to mumble all the way to and from the drinking fountain, setting the half-filled pans by the stove with a thud.

Jerome set the kettle on a burner, and put a griddle over two others. He invited the three to wash their hands and help cook. Rat ran to oblige. Luis mumbled again, but followed Ike's guiding tug. By the time they returned, Jerome had mixed a batch of lumpy pancake batter.

The four men huddled around the stove cooking sausages, eggs and pancakes. When the kettle came to a boil, Jerome dumped a heap of coffee into a paper filter.

"I figure we can put the filter over a cup and make coffee one cup at a time," he told Ike, proud of his logic.

"Haven't you ever made cowboy coffee?" Ike asked.

"I've never made *any* coffee," Jerome confessed.

"Put the kettle back on the stove."

He did, and Ike put three scoops of ground coffee into the boiling water.

"I see," said Jerome. "We'll strain the coffee when we pour it."

"Not exactly. Watch." Ike let the coffee boil a bit, then he poured a cup of cold water into the kettle and took it off the burner. The cold water made the coffee grounds settle to the bottom. Ike poured coffee into three cups Jerome put on the bench.

Soon other ragged people gathered on the outskirts of the park to watch the breakfast event.

"Okay, gentlemen. There are plates and forks in those bags. Eat up, we've got company." Jerome poured more coffee into additional cups he lined up along the bench, and invited the onlookers to come and partake. He then poured more water into the kettle to start a second round. As he cooked more pancakes, Jerome watched his friends wolf down breakfast. With each bite they took, both he and they became more full.

⁙

Bill, Boo and Harley left their apartment building for church. Seeing the gathering crowd, they went around the park instead of cutting through.

⁙

The rookie parked his squad car and approached the camp stove. Jerome glanced at him, but continued flipping flapjacks.

"Morning, Officer. Good to see you again."

The rookie first wrinkled his nose, staring for a moment before nodding. He cocked his chin up as a salutation. "Good to see you, too. You're looking better."

"And better looking."

The rookie surveyed the crowd. "You wouldn't happen to have a permit for this, would you?" he asked.

"Permit? No. Spatula, yes." Jerome handed his to the rookie and stepped aside. "You cook, I have to get more food." Before the rookie could protest he was at the stove tending bubbling raw pancakes.

Jerome hurried on foot to the corner store. From the street below he saw the roll-down iron covers still in place, but he continued to the store. As he tugged on the padlocks he heard a honk.

"Looking for me?" asked the owner from his car.

"Yes, as a matter of fact. Are you ready to open?"

"No, but I'm here. What do you need?"

"Food, and an address for those little girls."

"Food, I got. I didn't know you wanted an address. I never asked."

Jerome explained about the breakfast and the depleted supplies.

"Half off dated milk and bread," the owner offered, "and eggs two for one. Everything else is negotiable. Depends what it is."

Jerome quickly bought what was needed and hurried back to the park with arms loaded. People from the neighborhood were also bringing food. An old woman had joined the rookie and Ike at the stove, dishing oatmeal from a large aluminum pot.

The rookie introduced her. "This is Mrs. Dixon. She made mush."

"Thank you, Mrs. Dixon. That was very kind."

"You're welcome," she said. "When I saw Officer Curtis, I knew it was safe. It sure is chilly."

"It sure is. But you've made it warmer."

She grinned. Her upper denture plate dropped, nearly falling from her mouth. With a quick slurp she sucked it back.

The bench was now loaded with jugs of punch and milk, bread, cans, oranges, apples and bananas. A teen crossed the street with a bag of baby carrots, handing them to Rat.

"Not really for breakfast, but we figured you could use it."

"Most definitely," Rat answered. "We love carrots, don't we Luis?"

Luis mumbled something positive and placed the bag on the buffet bench where the homeless gathered like pigeons.

"Are we doing this next week?" asked Mrs. Dixon. "I could make sweet rolls."

"That's sounds good," answered the rookie. "I'll bring donuts."

"Won't you need a permit?" asked Jerome.

He admired the blind willingness. He only regretted that Annie wasn't there, having hoped she would show the way to the home of the man with crutches. By keeping his word to Ike, Jerome had blown his last chance to find Boo and Harley in time for Christmas.

"What do you think, Ike? You want to meet here next week?"

"Mi parque es su parque," said Ike, "but it will break your piggy bank."

"My piggy bank is safe. Look around. Food is coming from nowhere. The same thing will happen next week, and the next."

Jerome put his hands over the kettle, luring the heat into his gloves. On this cold Sunday morn, he was alive and cooking.

∽✿∾

It was after one o'clock before the camp stove was cool enough to load into the trunk. While Jerome finished packing his car, Rat and Ike chased breeze-blown trash across the park. Luis stood by grumbling until the last syrup-soaked plate was shoved into the garbage can.

Jerome removed his gloves to bid his friends good-bye with hand-shakes. When Luis tried to walk by without a word, Jerome tossed him the gloves.

"Here, Luis. One size fits all."

Luis caught the gloves, startled by the gesture. He put them on, curling his fingers for a good fit.

"Thanks," he said before running to catch Ike and Rat.

Jerome's car didn't get re-packed as neat or compact as when he came. The trunk and seats were cluttered with bags, dirty pots and utensils that rattled as he drove to the church.

The parking lot was empty. For a valiant cause Jerome had sacrificed an equally valiant cause.

The marquee now read:

WISE MEN WANTED   INQUIRE WITHIN

Jerome wasn't ready to admit defeat. He left his car to check the front doors. Both were locked. He pressed his forehead against the glass. In the dark foyer was a poster on an easel.

Children's
Christmas Pageant
Monday Evening
6:30 pm

Feeling a rush of relief and gratitude, Jerome exhaled a jubilant giggle. He had done the right thing without forfeiting his one last chance to find the girls.

He looked at the manger. The crèche was even more elaborately decorated for this, the week of Christmas. New straw had been laid as flooring. The wood frame beams were thickly wrapped with lengths of plastic holly. A foil star hung high on the wall of the church, with strands of mini-lights stretched as rays between it and the crèche.

Jerome swaggered to his warm car, pleased with himself. He removed his coat and stuffed it behind the driver's seat where it wouldn't get sticky from the cluttered mess. After yanking the shoulder belt across his chest, he slammed the door and sped away, mulling the events of the day, amazed by his own brilliance.

He had life licked.

He had Christmas in control.

He had slammed his coat sleeve in the car door. It whipped in the wind as a banner to his brilliance.

∽⊙∾

Jerome's wife was in bed asleep. The midnight hour approached. He stood on his back porch, wearing PJs under his coat with the tattered sleeve. There were no clouds to insulate the earth and hold any warmth. It was extremely cold.

Someone will die tonight, he thought, praying that Annie would be warm wherever she was. He hoped she had his comforter. Jerome hadn't needed her blanket as much as she needed his. He was barely two steps from comfort; she was barely two steps from death.

He felt a weight of responsibility like a lead-ball lei around his neck. Harley, Boo, their father, Ike, Annie, Rat, Luis, the woman and her two kids each needed something from him. There were others, including his wife and his students. Tomorrow he would return to school for the shortened pre-holiday week. He could no longer treat his students or his wife as invisible.

He said another prayer for Annie, nodding his amen to the star on the horizon before stepping inside to sleep in peace.

Jerome felt like a cat at a dog show. He stood at the lunchroom entrance with his class, waiting for Attila the lunch lady to wave them in. Here was where he usually ditched the kids for a private lunch, but not today. Attila gave the signal. Jerome patted each child on the back as they passed through the door, then he followed the last student to the utensil and tray rack.

Jerome flicked the dried whatever-it-was off the hot fork and put it on his tray with a napkin and spoon. Any residual microbes on the fork wouldn't kill him, though the corn dogs might. He felt his arteries clog just looking at them. After estimating the fat calories, he concluded it would be healthier to eat the stick.

"Have you any Grey Poupon?" Jerome asked Attila.

"Gray poop on what?" she answered, pointing to mustard packets in a bowl.

Jerome followed some of his students to a punk-sized table, squatting to sit on the low bench. At first they were embarrassed by his presence, but they got over it as he chattered about bugs and boogers. After diverting their attention, Jerome stuffed the corn dog in his milk carton so he could pass Attila's plate inspection.

"Did I ever tell you I once worked for a wiener?" he asked as they left to get their coats and head for the playground.

Jerome wandered around the tetherball pole and the hopscotch squares watching his children. He noticed his reflection off a classroom window and realized he was smiling so much that lines creased into his cheeks. Behind his reflection a flash of purple caught his eye. He turned to see a young girl running across the playground. It took a while to confirm that she was not Harley.

Jerome noticed other girls with purple coats, and yellow coats, and pink coats, and some with no coats at all. There were other Harleys all around him.

A girl tugged on his coat and handed him the hopscotch taw.

∽◦◦∽

He hadn't touched a taw since *the incident.*

Years ago a sixth-grade girl noticed a mild oniony odor on a day that

Jerome, in a rush to get to school, had forgotten to apply deodorant. Her whispers soon became boisterous group chants of *Pepé LePew! We smell you!* during recess. After a few weeks of harassment, Jerome began to watch for her in the halls, in the lunchroom, and at recess, but his direct and unwitnessed one-word reprimands did not dissuade her from initiating the group chants as he passed by.

After one particularly grueling day of teaching, Jerome noticed the instigator alone behind the school playing hopscotch. He crept up behind her as she hopped to the numeral *12*. When she turned to hop back, Jerome was standing at the *1* with her hopscotch taw in his hand.

"That's mine," she said.

"So?"

"Give it back!"

"It's mine now. You shouldn't have thrown it at the building."

"I didn't!"

"Yes you did. I saw you. It's mine now."

"I'll tell!"

"So? Who will they believe, Smartmouth? A little puke like you, or a teacher?"

Jerome could still see the mixed expression of anger and fear in her eyes. He could remember his fleeting thought that maybe they might believe her over him, and it maddened him that little girls wielded such power.

"Please give it back," she asked.

Jerome tossed it to her.

No, he finally admitted inside. He had tossed it *at* her, like an underhanded discus. The instant it left his fingers he regretted the act. It hovered across the ten numerals between him and her before it landed an uppercut to her lip, teeth and gum. He was at her side the moment the taw hit her.

"I'm sorry, I'm sorry!" he cried, but his pleading didn't stop the flow of blood and tears.

He, too, shed a few tears, more out of fear than remorse or empathy. He rushed her to the office with his sleeve against her lip to slow the bleeding. A secretary pressed a tissue to her mouth as Jerome rambled an explanation.

"She jerked the hoppy taw from my hand, and hit herself," he had said before running to the cafeteria for ice.

The girl's account was unintelligible through the tears and tissue, but eventually her version of the event was penciled into a report alongside his. A claim was filed. He objected, but his insurer and the school district paid her and her parents a nominal amount of hush money. The case was closed without anything negative put on his record, thanks to union pressure, but everyone on the faculty had their own opinion about what happened.

That was then. The instigator was now in high school. Jerome looked at the new taw in his hands, then at the student who gave it to him. She apparently hadn't heard about *the incident*. He rubbed the taw between his palms before stepping forward and dropping it inside the first square. He hopped to *12,* then walked away with his head down.

⚭

Jerome got home from school around 4:20. He set his keys on the kitchen counter, and saw the light on the phone message machine. He pressed PLAY.

"You have one new message," noted the electronic male voice before the beep.

"Jerome," said his wife's recorded voice. "I'm going to dad's place to tidy up. It would be nice if you could make it over. If I don't see you there, I should be home by seven. Think about pizza for dinner." *Beep.*

Jerome looked at his watch. Two hours before the church pageant, enough time for *Mayberry RFD.* He grabbed a knife, peanut butter and saltines, and sat in front of the TV to watch his favorite show. Then he watched *M*A*S*H* and the early news, munching on peanut brittle and chocolate-dipped pretzels for dessert.

Before Jerome departed for the pageant, he left a note on the fridge.

> Gone fishin'
> Didn't get a pizza. Had junk for dinner.
> I'll be home by 9?
> J.

⚭

Jerome made sure he arrived fashionably late, pulling into the church lot at 6:45 p.m. By arriving late he avoided a hand-shaking gauntlet of churchgoers. He saw no need to be early, since his best chance to meet the Edisons was after the pageant.

The number of cars in the lot surprised him. He hadn't expected a children's pageant to draw such a crowd.

The sky was dark and cloudless. It would be another cold night for Annie, wherever she was. Jerome stepped over an orange electrical cord that snaked across the sidewalk and snowy lawn to the crèche for the ground lights in front of the Holy Family. The lights cast rough-edged shadows against the church wall. The other end of the cord was pinched in the jamb of the front door, allowing Christmas melodies to tweak through the gap.

As he put his hand on the door, Jerome heard muffled voices singing *glorias.* The volume increased as the door opened. He let the door close against his hip to keep it from slamming against the cord.

An old woman at the chapel entrance reached out to greet him. "Come in, come in," she whispered, handing him a program. "Can I help you find a seat?"

"Let's have a look," he whispered back. "I see one over there, thanks."

He rolled the program into a tube, then ducked and waddled to a bench-end near the back. He scanned the stage for familiar faces. Two kids wearing bathrobes with towels on their heads were on the stage, but he saw neither Harley nor Boo. He looked over the backsides of more toweled heads. None of them looked familiar.

They should turn around when they sing, he thought, looking back at the chapel doors to make sure he had an easy escape. He visually scoured the other chapel occupants. He didn't see the man with crutches.

The song ended with an *in excelsus deo,* then the children sat on cue. A boy in a sheet toga joined the young couple on stage.

"Do you have any room at the inn?" the couple asked in unison. The innkeeper shook his head, but lead them to a corner of the stage decorated with a bale of straw.

The narrator read. "And Mary brought forth her firstborn son and wrapped Him in swaddling clothes, and laid Him in a manger because there was no room for them at the inn."

Jerome thought of Annie and her friends, now his friends. Their shelter was no better than a stable.

The chorister stepped forward and motioned. The children stood. *She should have put the small kids in back, and had them turn around,* he thought, refining his criticism. *How are we supposed to enjoy this?*

Mary wrapped a blanket around a baby doll and cuddled it through the song. During the final chorus she placed the baby on the hay, then she and Joseph knelt for the next song. The tune was familiar, but Jerome hadn't heard it since childhood. He unrolled his program to check the title.

When he looked up, a toweled head bobbed through a row of children. A pudgy-faced boy emerged at the aisle, his turban wedged onto his ears propping them out like gravy-boat handles. The boy gathered the hem of his oversized bathrobe and hurried up the aisle past Jerome, into the foyer and out of sight.

The children finished the song and were seated. The narrator paused as the next actors took their places. Jerome sat up with great interest to watch a girl with no towel on her head. She took the hand of a small, blue turbaned shepherd. Harley escorted Boo to a group of shepherds in the middle of the stage, then she went to stand by the chorister. A long quiet minute passed as everyone waited for the narrator to speak. Boo began to fidget. Harley gave her a shush signal.

From beyond the foyer came the distant sound of a toilet flushing. Within seconds the kid with big ears rushed through the chapel doors and down the aisle, his feet kicking the robe as he ran.

He's going to trip, he's going to trip, wished Jerome. But he didn't, safely reaching his place among the shepherds.

The narrator now continued. "And there were in the same country shepherds abiding in the field, keeping watch over their flock by night. And lo, the angel of the Lord came upon them, and the glory of the Lord shone round about them, and they were sore afraid. And the angel said unto them: Fear not! For behold, I bring you good tidings of great joy which shall be to all people. For unto you is born this day in the city of David, a Savior which is Christ the Lord. And this shall be a sign unto you: Ye shall find the babe wrapped in swaddling clothes, lying in a manger."

Jerome alternated watching Harley and Boo. Harley was somber and dignified. Boo just smiled, but her smile paled when compared with the goofy grin on the pudgy, big-eared shepherd beside her.

Boo looked in Jerome's direction. She smiled wider and waved. He almost waved back, but instead leaned into the aisle to peer around heads in front of him. Under a bench-end ahead, Jerome could see crutches partially protruding into the aisle.

"And suddenly there was with the angel a multitude of the heavenly host praising God, and saying: Glory to God in the highest, and on earth peace, good will toward men."

Harley stooped and raised a large glittered star high into the air. At the same instant, the chorister motioned for the children to stand. Without hesitation they began to sing. The first stanza tore at Jerome.

"*The first Noël the angels did say*
Was to certain poor shepherds in fields where they lay."

The words repeated in his mind. He thought of the angels and poor shepherds in his recent past, how they tended to him even though a stranger.

"*They looked up and saw a star*
Shining in the east that was so far."

Jerome alternated his gaze between the star, Harley and Boo, basking in the light of the moment, so glad to be there. Boo grinned and waved again, but her smile dissolved into a miffed pout when no one waved back.

The song ended all too soon. The children sat. Harley walked the star to Mary, Joseph and the Child. The shepherds followed her, except for Boo. She hopped down the carpeted steps and scampered to the bench where her father sat. He leaned into the aisle, and Boo kissed him on the cheek to the delight of all nearby.

Boo then walked to Jerome and waved in his face. "Halo, Sam's Club! Eye a chair bird foe Cheeses!"

Jerome dropped his tubed program. He tried to say something, anything. With blurring eyes, he watched Boo stroll back to the stage. His eyes met with those of her father glaring back at him. Jerome blinked rapidly to stay ahead of the gathering moisture. He couldn't smile, or nod, or offer any physical greeting to Boo's father, so he lowered his head until the man turned forward.

A tide of tears crumbled Jerome's composure like a splashed sandcastle. He escaped to the foyer, rushing to the outer doors to stare into the night beyond the glass.

Someone darted in front of a ground light outside, then someone else. Jerome heard them running on the crusty snow and immediately knew that the pranksters were at it again. He ran enraged through the door but was too late to give chase. The crèche had already been violated. Another cast member had joined Baby Jesus.

Next to the Child stood the cardboard cutout of Santa spraying deodorant under his arms.

Jerome wasn't sure how to react. For years he had played the part of this baseboard cutout, no more a symbol of Christmas than a pink flamingo or a birdbath.

The shadows of the Holy Family loomed large against the church wall. With his eyes, Jerome traced the outline of Joseph on the building. His shadow touched the foil star high on the wall. Jerome looked away from the foil star to search the horizon, finding the real star with little trouble. The bare branches of a tree obstructed his view. He tipped his head but couldn't get a clear view until he backed inside the wooden frame of the crèche. As he stepped back, the star seemed to rise above the tree.

Jerome now stood in front of the Santa cutout, the bright ground lights shining into his face. He held out his arm to shield his eyes as the congregation began to sing *O Come All Ye Faithful*. The star was positioned just above the tree and just below the holly trim wrapped around the wooden frame of the crèche.

A memory scorched his mind like brush fire. He looked from the star to the green plastic trim that decorated the wood frame.

"That wasn't ivy," he said. "It was holly."

The hair on his neck stiffened. His spine chilled. Shame hit him with a sucker punch to the gut. He gasped as his chest cinched tight, and panted foggy breaths to oxygenate his pounding heart, fighting not to sob.

He saw his error clearly. The decorative vines on the grave marker, pumpkin and *holly*, represented Laura Edison's daughters Boo and Holly.

Boo was born on Halloween, Holly on or near Christmas. Last year, Holly hadn't received a gift for either day, so Boo wanted something to give Holly for her birthday.

The singing grew loud.

"*Oh come let us adore Him,*
Christ the Lord."

Jerome surrendered to his gushing emotions. He bowed his head and wept, dabbing tears with his tattered coat sleeve. Through his moist eyes he stared at the star on the horizon glittering brighter than ever, emitting light strands from heaven to him.

"Help me help them," he prayed as he wiped his eyes and sniffed. He walked to his car to get the coin socks, looking away from the star as he reeled on an emotional precipice. After checking his appearance in the rear view mirror, he slapped his face and blinked his reddened eyes.

With socks in hand, Jerome again stepped through the church doors. The singing had stopped. People were pouring out of the chapel into the foyer, creating the gauntlet of fellowshippers he had hoped to avoid. Churchies were everywhere, some pausing to socialize, others weaving to the exit. Jerome sidestepped along the wall watching for Boo and Holly. In his mind he rehearsed several introductions.

"Hello. How are you?" said a man to Jerome's right. "My name is Marvin."

Jerome looked over to see a grown version of the goofy shepherd, complete with a towel turban. "I'm Sant—I'm Jerome."

"We haven't met before, but I'm new around here. It's a pleasure to meet you."

The pleasure's all yours, thought Jerome out of habit. "The pleasure is mine," he said. "Did you have a part in the pageant?"

"No. My son did. He was a shepherd, but he didn't want to wear a towel because he said it would look stupid. So I told him I would wear one if he would, to prove that he wouldn't look stupid."

Jerome wanted to say something, but he didn't. "Do you know the guy that does your sign out front? I think his last name is Edison."

"I don't know who does the sign."

"It's the guy with crutches."

"Oh. Okay. I know who you mean, but I don't know his name."

Young Marvin approached with his mother and brother.

"Jerome, I'd like you to meet my wife Etta, and our two boys Eldon and Marvin, Jr."

"Nice to meet you," Jerome nodded politely, shaking hands with young Marvin. His bathrobe was open and dragging on the floor. His fly was unzipped.

"Pssst. Marvin. XYZ," Jerome advised in a hushed voice.

Both Marvins examined their zippers. Etta rolled her eyes. Eldon laughed.

"Well, I better find Brother Edison," Jerome said excusing himself. "It was nice to meet you all." He looked inside the chapel but the girls and their father weren't there. Jerome hurried to the opposite foyer but saw no sign of them there, either.

"Have you seen the Eldons—I mean the Edisons?" he asked a woman by the kitchen.

"I think they just caught a ride," she answered, pointing to a push-bar exit. Jerome rushed through it to find back-lot parking. A car was turning the corner around the far side of the unlit lot, near the fenced playground. Jerome dashed back inside and ran down the hall, the socked coins chinking like a slot machine. He dodged standers and talkers in the halls, soon finding himself in the daycare foyer. He rushed past the empty coat rack through the side door.

The snow crunched under his feet as he raced across the lawn. The car nosed into traffic and accelerated away, leaving Jerome in the middle of the lawn. There was no time to get to his car and follow. He trotted back to the side door, out of breath, but found it locked. No one responded to the rap of his bare knuckle against the DAYCARE Matthew 7:7 sign.

Jerome felt a touch of warmth on his shoulder. He looked up and saw the star. There was still hope.

Returning to the front entrance, he asked around, but no one could tell him where the Edisons lived. He learned Bill's name, but found no one to confirm the names of Holly and Boo. He hung around the foyer until everyone was gone except an elderly couple with keys. When they turned off the lights, he left the chapel to sit in his cold car, and watched as the couple locked the doors and left.

Jerome stared at heaven, gazing at the star crawling across the sky, waiting and wishing for something to happen without knowing what.

Day Twenty-Eight, Tuesday

chool dismissed for the holiday break after a brief morning session of games and donuts. Jerome came home to an empty house just after noon, put on his comfortable checkered shirt, and sat at the kitchen table to check his gift list. It included Annie, Ike, Luis, Rat, the woman and her two children, the store owner, Mr. Ludwig and the photography elf. At the top of the list were Boo, Holly and Bill. Next to Holly's name were two check marks, one for Christmas and one for her birthday.

Jerome wanted to deliver gifts this afternoon, but he lacked an address for the Edisons. He thought about the church pageant, and the star, and the crèche, and the scripture on the daycare door, and tried hard to recall the verse and chapter as he rummaged through the desk drawer to find the pocket-sized Gideon's New Testament. He looked up Matthew 7:7.

"Ask, and it shall be given you; seek, and ye shall find; knock, and it shall be opened unto you."

Ask. Somehow he knew that Annie was back. He would ask her where Bill lived.

Seek. He would seek help from his wife. She had a good heart, and might think of something he hadn't considered.

Knock.

"Knock, knock."

"Who's there?"

"Boo."

Suddenly he *knew* where she was. The red-haired teacher didn't know her as Boo.

The doorbell rang. Jerome left the kitchen to answer the door. A deliveryman wearing a short-sleeve shirt, shorts and sockless tennis shoes stood on the porch, his bare arms and legs covered with goose bumps. He held a large brown box.

"From Chuckles' Clown Emporium," he said, handing Jerome the box and an electronic gizmo. "Sign here."

Jerome signed the gizmo and said thanks. He closed the door and read the bill of lading. It hadn't been shipped until Friday. He left the box by the door and started for the kitchen to get a knife, passing the tree loaded with ornaments. At its pinnacle was a bright aluminum star.

Jerome's body stalled while his mind raced. He twirled around, scooped up the package and rushed through the front door, jumping off the porch to run across the snow. He flagged the delivery truck as it backed into the street.

"Whoa, Nellie! Hold up! Take this back to Chuckles. I don't need it anymore."

The deliveryman took the package and tossed it in back, then again punched gizmo buttons. He handed it to Jerome.

"Unsign here."

Jerome did. He strolled houseward, stretching and flexing his spine like a spring moth leaving its cocoon. He finally had all the right answers.

He knew who he was.

He had been a good boy.

He knew what he wanted for Christmas.

Hurrying inside, Jerome stuffed wrapped packages into plastic bags and then into his car. Before leaving he paused at the kitchen table to write a quick note.

> Gone fishin' again.
> Off to land the catch of a lifetime.
> I'll explain when I get home, probably around 6.
>   J.

Jerome set the pen beside the note and re-read it. It—and he—seemed incomplete without a postscript. He picked up the pen.

> P.S. I sure do love you.

Boo sat at a tiny desk in the classroom nearest the daycare foyer, carefully coloring with a white crayon. She had positioned her chair on the wrong side of the desk so she could watch the door.

"Can I see your picture, Marci?" asked the red-haired teacher.

"Eye knot dung whiff ick," she answered.

"It is really pretty. Is it a Christmas picture?"

"Uh-huh."

"Who is this?" asked the teacher, pointing to the largest character in the center. "Is that you?"

"No! Hats Bevy Cheeses."

"Oops, sorry. Then this is Mary?"

Marci nodded.

"And this is Joseph?"

"No," she huffed, pulling the paper to her chest. "Fats Scab Clots!"

Boo protectively leaned over her artwork to put the final touches on Santa's fake beard. She then dropped the white crayon into the box and rummaged for just the right colors to finish Santa's checkered shirt.

⚜

Jerome knocked on the daycare door as he stepped over the threshold with a garbage bag full of wrapped gifts. "Anybody home?" he said loudly.

"No, we're all here at the daycare," he and the red-haired teacher answered in unison. The teacher smiled at their joint response.

"I came back for Boo Edison," Jerome said. "You must know her by some other name." He showed the teacher his Polaroid snapshot of Boo squirming off Santa's lap.

"Marci. Her name is Marci. You missed her and her sister by five minutes."

"Holly?"

"Yeah."

"Were they going to the mall? Or were they going home? If you know."

"I don't know. They usually meet their dad at the bus stop, but today Holly came with her aunt."

"Her aunt?"

"That's my guess. I know she wasn't her mom, so I'm guessing an aunt or something. They all left in her car."

"Any chance they have a phone?"

"Nope."

"Then I need the their address."

"I'm sorry, I can't."

"See this bag? It's their Christmas. I need to deliver this stuff to them."

"I'm sorry, but I don't know you from Adam. I *do* know that we're doing a sub-for-Santa for them. Marci and Holly won't go without Christmas."

"When are you going to deliver your presents?"

"This evening."

"Can I tag along?"

"I'd have to think about that. If I can't tell you where they live, it seems worse to take you there."

Jerome stopped talking for a moment, listening to quiet echoes from the hall. His real concern was that the girls receive the gifts, not that he be there to give them.

"If I leave these with you, will you deliver them?"

"Sure. Why not?"

"Great. But if I find the girls on my own, I'll come back for them. Capisce?"

"That's only fair. But I won't be here too much longer."

"What time are you leaving?"

"Four o'clock."

Jerome looked at his watch. He had two hours to find the Edisons. *So much for Knock*, he thought.

❧❀❧

The sky was clear and blue. Jerome waited in his car parked near the broken pay phone, watching for Annie to return to the urban cave one half block away. A black car with tinted windows repeatedly circled the park, slowing each time it got close to Jerome. It cruised the block like a programmed mouse in a maze. With the hovering black vulture, Jerome felt safer parked in the open instead of down the block in front of Annie's dark haven. He kept his car in gear, ready to speed away if necessary.

Finally Annie appeared, cutting through the park on a well trodden snowway. She held a bag with one hand, and with the other she clutched her ragged black shawl close to her neck. Jerome sat up and waved, trying to get her attention so he wouldn't have to leave the warmth and imagined safety of his car. When she didn't respond, he reluctantly stepped out and hurried toward her.

"Annie! Annie!" he called, jogging across the packed snow. She kept her head down, pretending to ignore him but peeking side-eyed at him. Only after she recognized him did she look up.

"Well, well! You got your sea legs back!"

"Yeah, I'm feeling chipper. I came back for another heaping helping."

"You want me to give it to ya?" she asked, lifting her bag with a curled fist to shake at him. "You ain't had no whippin' till you had one from me."

"I'll pass. How were your boys?"

"They're fine. Real fine."

"They get that from their mom. Nuts don't fall far from the tree." His proverb wasn't as complementary as intended. "I meant peaches. Peaches don't fall far from the tree."

"I know what ya meant," she answered, smiling. "You meant I was crazy, and my boys was fruits."

"Did you get the blankets?"

"Yeah, thank you. They're very nice and warm."

"I worried about you. I also got you something for Christmas."

"You didn't have to do that."

"Yes, I did. I owe you . . . a lot. And, I need another favor. Remember that night you helped the guy with crutches?"

"How'd you know about that?"

"I watched the whole thing. I was too big a jerk to stop and help. But you weren't."

"Is that s'posed to be another compliment?"

"It *was*. I need to know where the man lives."

"He won't need no apology. You didn't know better."

"I wasn't really planning to apologize. I also got him and his daughters some things for Christmas."

"They live right there." Annie pointed past his car and the broken pay phone.

"Right there? This whole time?"

Annie nodded. Jerome followed her along another snowway leading to the apartment building.

"This is how I got beat up, looking for them."

"You shoulda asked."

"I shoulda."

Stepping into the building and climbing the stairs made Jerome feel like he had died and gone to Heaven. Annie stopped at the first door.

"This is it," she said.

Jerome inhaled before knocking *shave and a haircut* on the heavily painted door. He heard nothing from inside. He knocked the same cadence and added *two bits*. A door down the hall creaked. Jerome winked at the eye in the gap.

"They moved," said an elderly voice from the gap.

"Who moved?" Jerome questioned.

"Bill," answered the voice with a slurp.

Jerome had heard the voice before. "Mrs. Dixon? Is that you?"

The door opened a little wider. Mrs. Dixon poked her head through. "How did you know my name?"

"The park. Sunday. Pancakes and mush. Remember?"

Annie spoke up. "I heard 'bout the mush. It wasn't very good."

Jerome turned toward Annie and shaped his lips into a *shhh*, rolling his eyes to point at Mrs. Dixon. Annie's eyes widened.

"No, it wasn't *good*," she proclaimed. "It was great, the best mush they ever had!"

"Are you sure they moved?" Jerome asked Mrs. Dixon.

"I watched them carry their things out. Then the girls came over to say good-bye."

"Do you know where they went?"

Mrs. Dixon shook her head *no*.

"Do you know if they're coming back for anything?"

Mrs. Dixon again shook her head. "I don't think so. It sounds like they're moving to a palace."

"What do you mean?"

"Holly said they get beds and a dresser and a kitchen and a backyard. They must have won the lottery."

"Who's going to pick up their mail?"

"The super, maybe. He lives in the basement."

Jerome stepped around Annie and went down the stairs. He rang the bell of the door marked MANAGER, and received a quick response to his inquiry.

"No, they aren't coming back."

"Are you positive?"

"I got their key. They had to clean up or forfeit their deposit. So Bill looks at his girlfriend, she nods, and so he hands me the key. He's whipped already."

"Bill's got a girlfriend?"

"I'll say! Drop-dead gorgeous, too. How's he get a woman like that? You got me."

"No forwarding address?"

"Nope."

"Did they say they'd come back and clean up for the deposit?"

"Nope."

"How much was it?"

"Fifty bucks."

"He walked away from fifty bucks?"

"He sure did. I told him if the place wasn't cleaned by six, adios deposit."

"What's left to clean?"

"Scrub the toilet, dump the garbage, mop the floor. I guess him and his girl couldn't lift the trashy mattresses."

"And you couldn't help?"

The manager smiled. "I got a bad back."

Jerome paused in thought. "Fifty bucks?" he asked. "If I clean the place, can they have their deposit back?"

"I don't care who cleans it. But *they* have to come get the deposit. I ain't giving it to you."

"Of course. Give me the key."

Jerome hurried back upstairs to Annie and Mrs. Dixon. He inserted the key and turned the deadbolt lock. He pushed the door open and reached for the light switch, clicking it up and down.

"Is there a power box that's shut off?"

"No," answered Mrs. Dixon. "They didn't have electricity for months."

"Months?"

Mrs. Dixon nodded.

"What about heat?"

"They had heat."

Jerome, Annie and Mrs. Dixon filed into the apartment. The only things left were two dirty mattresses on the floor, a box of trash, and a piece of cardboard in the window.

"Mrs. Dixon, can I borrow a broom, and a mop and bucket?" Jerome asked as he stepped to the window and removed the cardboard. He pressed his face against the glass to view his car, the pay phone, and the site of his ambush. His breath clouded the cold pane.

"Boo and Holly are all right," he heard his inner voice say. *"You worry about cleaning up."*

"There's not much here," Jerome answered aloud. "Just a little clutter."

"Then clear the clutter."

As the fogged pane evaporated to opaque, Jerome thought he saw a twinkle in the afternoon sky. He heard angelic voices singing in the hallway.

"*Hark! The herald angels sing.*
Glory to the newborn King!
Peace on earth, and mercy mild,
God and sinners reconciled."

The singing slowly ended like an unwinding music box. Jerome turned from the window to greet the carolers at the open apartment door. At the front of the group, the red-haired teacher stood with a confused look on her face, clutching his bag of presents.

"They moved," Jerome said, easing his bag from the red-haired teacher's grasp. "I'll take these."

❧☙

Jerome left one mattress leaning against the dumpster behind the apartment building, just in case Ike, Rat or Luis wanted it. He set the better mattress on the roof of his car, then slowly drove with Annie to the urban cave. Annie steadied the mattress on the fence while Jerome squeezed through to the other side, then he lifted it over and carried it to the plywood-covered entrance. Annie held the plywood open as Jerome tugged the mattress inside. He didn't even try to adjust his eyes to the dim.

"I'll be right back," he said, hurrying to his car to get the gifts for his homeless friends. He dropped their bag of goodies over the fence, squeezed through again, and returned to Annie. "These are for Christmas morning. Maybe you could hide them, and set them out when everyone's asleep."

"That'd be fun," Annie commented. "You ever think 'bout doin' this for a living?"

"Nah! There are candy canes and chocolates in there, for your stockings."

During the brief lull, Jerome began to think. *"Clean up,"* he instructed himself, looking around at the challenge.

"Maybe we should tidy up a bit, for Christmas," he said to Annie.

"Everybody should tidy up for Christmas. That's what Christmas's all about."

With that said, Jerome began to clean.

❧☙

Jerome was a grungy mess when he dragged a bag of presents up three flights of stairs to the woman and her two children. He hadn't noticed the depth of filth on his hands until he began knocking.

"Tidy up. That's what Christmas is all about."

"Who is it?" the woman asked through the door.

"The third Wise Man," he answered. "I'm here with the myrrh."

She opened the door a crack.

"These are from the two little girls," he said, trying to gain her confidence. He opened the garbage bag to reveal his wrapped gifts. "By the way, you wouldn't happen to know their new address, would you?"

The woman shook her head *no.*

"They didn't move in with you, did they?" he asked. The woman didn't appear drop-dead gorgeous to Jerome, but beauty was in the eye of the beholder.

The woman shook her head again.

"Tidy up!" Jerome thought.

"Mind if I borrow your sink to wash my hands?" he asked.

The woman nodded *yes* and closed the door.

"Okay. I can take a hint," he said with his mouth against the door. "Just don't leave this stuff in the hall when I'm gone."

৩৩৩৩

Jerome stepped from the dusk across the threshold of the corner store. He walked toward the register and set a small wrapped box on the counter.

"What's this?" asked the store owner.

"Just something to say thanks, and Merry Christmas."

The owner picked up the box and weighed it in his hand, shaking it lightly.

"Open it," Jerome encouraged. "It's nothing, really. Mind if I use the little boy's room to wash my hands?"

"In the back, through the double doors," answered the owner, nodding up the aisle. He began to pick tape off the folded edge of the wrapping as Jerome stepped toward the back room.

Jerome stood over the sink, looking in the mirror at the grime on his face. The dirt was powdery gray, almost invisible in the dim light from the low watt bulb. He grabbed the soap and spun it under the stream of water to work up a lather. A flowery fragrance rose to his nostrils as bubbles multiplied in his palms. He scrubbed and rinsed his hands twice before washing and drying his face.

Jerome re-inspected his reflection. He stared himself in the eyes, unconvinced that his cleanup was complete, particularly after the soap's pleasant fragrance surrendered to a stench. He checked the bottom of his shoe.

"Great!" he said.

He back-tracked along a patchy trail of gooey marks left by his every-other footstep, tip-toeing on his fouled foot to avoid further soiling. The closer he got to the store exit, the thicker were the marks. The owner stood behind the counter, shaking his new snow globe to brew another storm. He spoke without looking up.

"Thanks for the gift. Mop's in the bathroom. You made the mess, you clean it."

"I didn't actually *make* the mess," Jerome said as he hobbled out the exit. "I'll be right back."

He stepped to the curb to cleanse his sole.

⁍⊙⊙⋖

Jerome didn't have time to hang around the North Pole. He gave the photography elf a wrapped snow globe, bid him a Merry Christmas, and left in a flash. He didn't stay long with Mr. Ludwig either, handing off another wrapped snow globe like a football to a halfback.

He hurried to make his final mall delivery. Pulling a folded paper from his pocket, he pressed on the creases to make it easier to slide under the door. He had penned the note in his car, writing what he didn't dare to speak.

> Moreen and Werner,
> Sorry I missed you.
> I dropped by to apologize for things
>   that may have caused you offense.
> Merry Christmas,
>   Jerome
>
> P.S. I'm not trying to get the Santa job back.

Jerome crouched at the mall management entrance and slipped the folded paper into the tight gap under the door. Suddenly, it opened inward, sweeping the paper from his fingertips.

"Jerome, what are you doing?"

He stood up. "Hello, Moreen. I was passing by and saw this piece of trash by the door. I was just about to pick it up."

He bent to reach for the note, but Moreen put her foot on it.

"I'll get it," she said, stooping.

She opened the note and rotated it right-side-up, then quietly read it before folding it again.

"And a Merry Christmas to you, Jerome. Your not coming back is the best Christmas gift ever," she said.

"'Tis better to give than to receive," Jerome countered. He turned away, but stopped a few paces from the door. "Moreen? Can I have that pink coat? I'd like to return it to the little girl."

"The coat is history. Mr. Charles discarded it after he finished his investigation."

"Did he find the girl?"

"No. The coat was a dead end."

"Did you keep the address in the coat? I'd like to go by there myself, if you don't mind."

"I don't have the address. You'll have to ask Mr. Charles next week."

"Maybe I'll call him. I'll see how it goes. Thanks, Moreen. See you around."

Jerome wandered through the mall to the parking lot. Walking to his car, chin up, he stared at the dark, cloudless sky scattered with stars. He inserted the key but didn't open the car door. Instead he paused to look over his shoulder at the eastern horizon. He listened with his eyes. There was yet one more chore to finish before going home.

He went back inside the mall to find a stuffed skunk.

***

The concrete porch steps were slicked by crystalline ice formed by the cold, humid air. Jerome checked the name on the mailbox as he scraped his feet on the doormat. The mailbox matched the phonebook address: *R. TAYLOR.*

Despite the chill of the night, Jerome's bare hands were warm and clammy. The moisture streamed in the creases of his palm as he clutched the shopping bag filled with three items: a Hallmark card, a stuffed Pepé LePew, and a hopscotch taw. The glee of finding the last two items was now gone. Jerome wished he could tidy this mess some other day far in the future. He watched his finger point outward, unable to keep it from pressing the doorbell.

The porch light came on. The instigator opened the door. In some other venue he might not have recognized her. She had matured since Jerome last saw her, but her lip still had an ever-so-slight mark where the hopscotch taw had hit her.

"Hello, Suzy. Is your mom or dad home?"

"Just a minute." She closed the door. Jerome wished he had asked only for her mom, as he did not want to face her father. The door opened again.

"Hello, Mrs. Taylor. I'm sorry to interrupt whatever you were doing, especially at this late hour. I have something to deliver to Suzy, and thought you should hear it, too."

Jerome's greeting received no immediate reply. Background piano music from the *Charlie Brown Christmas Special* puttied the gap in conversation, but the verbal silence remained awkward.

"May I come in, just for a minute?" he asked.

Mrs. Taylor glanced at Jerome's hair, his neck, his chin, his shoulder, anywhere except his eyes. After a long internal debate she spoke.

"For a minute."

She stepped back, letting him enter.

Jerome stopped in the doorway, clutching the shopping bag with both hands. He hesitated to ask another question, but knew he had to.

"Is your husband home? He probably ought to hear this as well."

"He's no longer around. What you have to say can be said to me and Suzy."

She stood beside her daughter, her hand on Susy's waist. Mrs. Taylor now looked Jerome in the eyes as he looked away. He was a bird in a guilted cage. He began to cry as he fumbled for words.

"I have done a lot of rotten things in my life, but I can't think of anything worse than what I did to Suzy. I was wrong. I was wrong to take the hopscotch marker. I was wrong to throw it. I made it worse when I lied about it. I'm sorry I lied. I'm really sorry about the scar on the lip. Even if no one else ever notices, I can see it. And I know she sees it every day, and will for a long time." Jerome wiped his eyes and handed the bag to Suzy. "I'll fix my statement after the Christmas break, and have them re-evaluate the claim. I'll do whatever it takes to make it right."

Suzy peeked into the bag and suppressed a grin. "Pepé LePew," she said.

"Who, *me?*" asked Jerome.

⸙

Jerome unlocked the house door, and entered his quiet home through the kitchen. It was after 8 o'clock. The Christmas tree lights from down the hall illuminated the kitchen enough for Jerome to see where he was going without flipping a switch. He carried his bag of undelivered gifts through the kitchen, and set them beside the tree before returning to find something to eat. Flipping the light switch, he strolled to the refrigerator where he found lasagna on a plate wrapped in cellophane.

Although the food was still warm to his touch, it needed a booster shot. He put the plate in the microwave and set the timer for 33 seconds.

His wife's note was beside a drawing on the kitchen table. Picking it up, he sped-read the first lines.

> J—
> I waited as long as I could.
> I'm at dad's place.
> There's lasagna in the fridge.

The microwave beeped. He put the note down to get a fork and a glass of milk. As he set the table, service for one, he read the rest of his wife's note.

> I took dinner to our new tenants.
> They're really nice and needed some help.
> I think you'll like them.
>   Robbie

Jerome scooted the note aside to examine the drawing, a crayon picture of Jesus, Mary, and a Wise Man in a checkered shirt.

erod lay restless on his bed. The silent night tormented the delusionary old king with a deep fear of insurrection. This was *his* kingdom, *his* dominion, *his* palace. No child of another would take his throne peaceably.

He heard the chink of metal against stone, then a plop into the still water of the fountain. He jumped from his bed screaming in terror.

"In the garden! He has come!"

Guards rushed through the bedchamber. They searched around the fountain, then behind the shrubbery and along the tall inescapable walls. They found no intruder.

Herod ordered the guards to repeat the search, convinced that someone had invaded his sanctuary. When again nothing was found, he dismissed them and sat at the fountain's edge to stare at the moon's reflection on the smooth surface of the shallow green water.

A glint of yellow caught his eye. He tilted his head to look at the refracted amber light. Without drawing back his sleeve, Herod reached into the water to retrieve a gold coin laying on the moss.

He knew the man from the East would not return.

⚜

On a grassy hill far from Jerusalem, Melchior and his servant stared at the myriad of stars. Although some were visibly brighter, none was internally brighter than the one.

"Lord, the star can be seen by all. Why did we alone follow? Are there no others who believe?"

Melchior responded. "It is written:

> *The wise shall shine bright as if stars in the heavens,*
> *Turning many to excellence, forever and ever.*

"We are not alone, Ben-Amalek. Look. The star is as bright tonight as the last. There will be others in distant lands and times who will see the star, hear its voice, and follow its light. They, too, will find Christ among the poor. They, too, will give in honor of His birth. But the truly wise will reconcile their lives, and receive the greatest gift of all—forgiveness."

The words gave Ben-Amalek a feeling of serenity and peace. "Master, wherever the star may guide, I will gladly follow."

"*We* will, my friend. With gladness, we will."